JOURNEY *to* TOMORROW

JOURNEY *to* TOMORROW

A NOVEL

DANIEL HILL ZAFREN

Published by Time Treasures Books, Goose Creek, South Carolina
www.timetreasuresbooks.com

ISBN: 978-1-7345129-1-5

Cover and interior by Susan Newman Design Inc.

The earlier books by Daniel Hill Zafren:

In a World We Never Made (2001)
A Door Never Opened (2003)
Shadow Selves (2005)
Network of Death (2006)
Not Lost – Just Not Found (2008)
Restless Beauty (2009)
Glimpses of Forgotten Dreams (2010)
Echo in the Heart (2011)
Double Hugs (2011)
Page Passage (2013)
Wish Winds (2014)
Unfinished Thinking (2015)
Vain Regrets (2016)
Network Secret (2016)
Forever Old, Forever New (2017)
Endless Time (2018)
A Gray Voyager (2019)
Right Sight (2020)

When I can look life in the eyes,
Grown calm and very coldly wise,
Life will have given me the Truth,
And taken in exchange – my youth.

– Sara Teardale

ONE

It was just a dream, but it seemed so real. He was given the chance to go back and relive a certain chosen period of time. Would it be to capture a lost love, to undo a major mistake, to make a different choice when the option was there, or to salve a hurtful gesture or action to another?

Life, whether it be in a dream or reality, is complicated. We like to think we can make it just what we want it to be, but at the end of the day life controls us rather than we controlling it. It seems too often the vagaries of life dominate even when thinking and planning are clear and precise. Understanding it all is just another exercise in futility.

For Thomas Lloyd dreams represented an additional challenge. Now that he was in the winter of his life the dreams became more puzzling and frustrating, easily transferring to unsettled feelings in his waking hours. The dreams had always been vivid and detailed, and the older he became the more baffled he was about some of the things he dreamed about. A degree of uncertainty arose whether some of the scenes actually happened, in whole or in part. A number of times over the years he had dreamed he had gone to work for an international insurance company before he had started practicing law. That company recognized his abilities early on and elevated him into a newly created managerial position. There was a rewarding feeling of accomplishment in the projects he headed and he became closely reliant on a number of dedicated employees. Such led to many a dream debate as to whether he had made the right choice in leaving the company for a law practice. Had it actually happened that way? Research on the company revealed that it had actually existed although it had been absorbed by another company more than twenty years ago. Employee records were inaccessible. Tax returns are destroyed by IRS after six years.

Besides the blurring of lines between reality and dreams, another mental battle an elderly person gets absorbed in is the memory of a person or event. The intervening years between the then and the now are bound to affect what was remembered and its interpretation. A thinker thinks too much. That is why he is a thinker, and mental skirmishes usually lead to emotional unease.

So, here he was in his retirement years, and instead of calm and relaxing days his restless spirit was constantly grappling with what had been, what might have been, and what should have been. He tried a number of times to explain the quagmire to April, his wife, and there was little doubt she was exasperated and impatient with him. It was not the first time in their sixty-two year marriage that his imagination had produced mountains from ant hills. The sage woman learned long ago to just listen to his ranting and eventually he would wear himself out or get distracted elsewhere. Yet, it was not an easy exercise for her. Her perpetual advice which she followed herself to live a satisfied life was to just accept things as they are. Once you question the nature of the bumps in the road the trip can no longer be totally satisfying. A lesson he refused to learn.

A further discontent was from the disconnect. You would think that at least a few of the friends they made when they moved to the retirement community in Hilton Head would also have such disquieting thoughts. If there were any, he had yet to find them. If in conversation he brought up the point that old age is not a destination of the life trip but merely a rest stop and that each day is vital because it is the journey to tomorrow, blank stares and mumbling of a noncaring outlook would quickly lead to an abandonment of the subject.

He was not surprised or dismayed that he was this way. He had been a mental loner all of his life. He shunned group activity as a youngster. He declined to join a fraternity in college. He would not choose a religion. April was pretty much the same way when he met her, so there was a degree of comfort in joint thoughts and activities. Over the years she lost much of this mental independence, and he attributed that to the friends she gravitated to who were fashion conscious and celebrity influenced. Once the children were grown and out on their own, the mutual nurturing role went away as well. The children and their families cared about the old folks and kept in touch, but they were so involved in busy lives of their own there seemed to be little room for sharing of lives and ideas. One Christmas, just to see if he was listening, he told his son, Alex, that he had become suicidal. Alex chuckled and responded that at his age he should try to be more serious. That spoke volumes.

So, was he a loose cannon? Or, did he just have a screw loose? And the big question – what was he going to do about it?

TWO

Tom was not surprised that the answer came to him in a dream. While the subjects of the dreams were generally haphazard, situations that arose were usually handled in an orderly fashion. For an old person, orderly fashion is as good as it gets.

He was not retiring from life. He was retiring from retirement. For all he knew it was as cockeyed as it sounded. Yet, as far as he could figure it, a compulsion to go back to work had taken a firm hold on his destiny. Yes, even an old person has a destiny besides death. What kind of work can an elderly person do? Certain categories were available and appeared to be socially acceptable, such as a greeter at WalMart, a bagger at the supermarket, or a driver at the auto auction. That was not for him. He would branch out to new territory. Over the years, there were situations in his dreams where he was called on to do an investigation. Hooking on that, he would become a senior private investigator for seniors. Through conversations and observations, it was evident that seniors might need such a service and would find it more comfortable with a contemporary filling the need. Genuine understanding and empathy would be present. His humorous side even contemplated that if the operation did not take off, he could easily convert the business to a senior male escort service. There were lots of lonely old ladies out there who would welcome a rental companion. Of course, the physical aspects of any amorous adventure would be quite limited or even completely unattainable.

The two word reaction from April was as he would have predicted it. "Good grief!" Yet, she knew better than to be adamant about the venture. That would fuel his plan. It was just another off-the-beaten-path notion he had to get out of his system. The idea had flickered through her mind more than once over recent years that she should probably leave him and find a normal man, if such an animal actually existed. After all, these years were supposed to be tranquil rather than a series of upheavals emanating from half baked ideas. A secret of old age is that there has to be more than physical comfort in the final countdown.

It only took two weeks to get a license from the State to conduct such a business and, of course, getting a tax number so the State could reap a benefit. He also made sure the license for him to carry a concealed weapon was up-to-date. He had such a license for over thirty years, ever since a disgruntled client had made a subtle threat on his life. The firearms training required to get the license was valuable, and it evoked the memory as a boy when he wanted to become a policeman.

The major problem was finding an office to work out of. There was a row of convenience stores right in the retirement community but they were all rented. A larger strip shopping mall across the highway would have to do. A small store was available although he thought the rent rather high. He would have to keep that in mind when he set his fees. Basic furniture and furnishings also put a dent in their bank account. Utilities and telephone were also necessary.

Six weeks later, and after a mass mailing announcing the opening of the business to his retirement community as well as the other adult communities in the Hilton Head area, the office was open. For two weeks all was quiet. No visits and no calls, not even from well wishers. It confirmed his perception that the friends were of the mind that he was out of his mind. April did not even come by, and he interpreted that as a further way of showing her disapproval. It was a good thing he had a stack of books to read to pass the time. He was nearly finished with the eighth book when a knock on the door interrupted him. The door was unlocked, and there was a sign on it that said to just enter. What he saw was not what he expected. Instead of a silver-haired senior, it was a petite young woman. He was sitting at the desk and motioned for her to come in. Slowly, she opened the door and sat in the chair in front of the desk that he pointed to. "What can I do for you, young lady?"

Her long black hair cascaded around her shoulders. Wide black eyes peered at him under the bangs. For an instant he thought it quite unfair that young people do not have bags under their eyes. He noted she was wearing an apron over her jeans and blouse. She smiled showing the universal status from the orthodontist world of perfect teeth. "Nothing." Her voice was soft and clear. "I just wanted to see what a real private eye looks like."

He laughed, realizing it had been far too long since he had done so. "I'm no Mannix, and a P. I. can look like anyone."

Her tone was mellow, almost tantalizing. "I work part time in the florist next door. I'm on break and just have been busting to come in here."

"I hope you are not disappointed. I'm an old buzzard on a mission."

"I'm a young hen on an adventure."

Again, he laughed. "You are an amusing youngster."

"You haven't heard anything yet."

"Oh!"

"I want to be a private investigator."

He wanted to laugh but restrained himself. "And, why is that?"

"I think it would be more exciting than making floral

arrangements."

"And I would think doing that is more engaging, and certainly more lucrative. I haven't had a client since I opened."

She smiled, and it was a warm smile. "I thought old folks prided themselves on their patience. They'll come. I have overheard customers talking about you."

He smiled back displaying the costly dentures. "See, you are already investigating."

"You are the Thomas Lloyd on the store front?"

"In the flesh. I am a living legend."

"Do you want me to call you Thomas, Tom, or Mr. Lloyd?"

"Any of the above."

"I think I'll call you Tommy."

"I haven't been called that since I was a boy. But, it does have a nice ring to it. You call me whatever moves you. What is your name?"

"Michelle Greenmore, but everyone calls me Mac."

"How so?"

"When I was a little girl all I wanted to eat was macaroni and cheese."

"You are still a little girl."

"If you think that you are not a good gum shoe. Guess how old I am?"

"Nineteen, tops."

She giggled. "Try twenty-seven."

"No way. When I was twenty-seven people thought I was fifty."

It was her turn to laugh. "How old are you now?"

"Too old for you."

She laughed again. "I like mature men."

"I'm way past mature. Try ancient. I've had macaroni and

cheese for eighty-two years."

"Wow! You don't look a day over eighty-one. You look good for your age."

He liked her spunk. It made him feel younger. "Age is experience and outlook."

"Wise, too. Look, I have to get back to the flowers. I'll stop in again when I am finished."

"O.K. Bring some friends with you that have problems calling for a detective."

"I have no friends." She sounded serious.

"You have one now."

THREE

True to her word, Mac returned early in the afternoon. She knocked again but entered right away without any direction from Tom. Without the apron, he noted her full figure on the petite frame. She sat in the chair before the desk. "Do you like what you see?"

"If only I were a young man. Do you have a boyfriend?"

"Boyfriends are a waste of time and energy. Life is too short for such nonsense."

"Now, who is being wise?"

"I have a deal for you, Tommy, and you better say yes."

"Yes."

She laughed. "Not yet."

"Oh!"

"After work at the florist each day, I'll come here and be your Secretary and Assistant. The place is small but I think you can fit in another desk. You will pay me 25% of whatever you make, and pay me under the table so you don't have to withhold anything or go through the complications of having an employee."

"And, young lass, why would I want to do this?"

"People will think you are a true professional and doing well if you have a Secretary and Assistant."

"What people?"

"They'll come if for no other reason than to see your sexy Secretary."

"And what if I say no?"

"I'll picket your office and tell people who want to come in that you are too old and feeble to help them."

"I'll have them come in while you are working in the florist shop."

"Then I'll catch them on the way out."

"Insistent, aren't you?"

"I know what I want."

"You are too young to understand that."

"You would be surprised."

"I would be, and during our many quiet moments you can explain it to me."

"You are supposed to be teaching me, not the other way around."

"I suspect there are things I can learn from you as well."

"See, you are already learning from me."

"Are you sure this is what you want to do?"

"Yup."

"Alright, we'll try it for two months. Promise me one thing, though."

"What is that?"

"You will not try to seduce me."

"And, vice versa......unless I want you to."

He laughed this time. "I don't see that ever happening, but miracles do occur."

"Have you ever experienced a miracle first hand?"

He thought for a moment. "Not in the sense that you mean, although I suppose it is a miracle I wake up in the morning and can get out of bed."

She giggled. "I don't really believe in miracles. Sure, you can put a label on all sorts of unusual events but it is all just as the ball in life bounces."

"You are too young to be a cynic."

"And you are too old not to be one."

"Then, we are even."

She handed him a sheet of paper. "Here is my full name, address, and cell phone number. Call me when you need me to do the physical things an old man is strained to do."

"That is why I have a urologist."

She laughed loudly. "Pursuits, stake outs, travel, you name it. You will find I am completely trustworthy."

"I hope so. I am taking a chance on you."

"And, I am taking a chance on you. As I learn, my safety and well being are in your hands."

"That's a tall order."

"If I didn't think you could do it, we wouldn't be having this conversation. Anyway, I live with my mother so I have to go home and check on her. We'll start when you get the desk."

"We'll start when I get a client."

She came around the desk. "No, I am not going to sit in your lap. Let's seal the deal with a hug."

He stood up and realized as he put his arms around her she barely came up to his chin. Even if there was no business, he had the feeling just having her around would be good for his spirits. Old people should have a constant youthful presence around them. It is a win-win situation.

When he told April about Mac, she let out a long sigh. "I hope you know what you are doing, but I doubt it. You are hardly able to be responsible for yourself. What makes you think you can also be responsible for a young woman?"

The words clarified what he had been thinking. "She is no ordinary woman."

FOUR

Mac felt she was getting some place at last. She was finally going to do something she wanted to do rather than one she had to do. Life had been a series of mishaps and uncertainties since she had graduated from high school. The classes at the community college were dull and left her unchallenged, and it was a wonder she lasted there for a year. Odd jobs were taken not because she was interested in them but because they were available. She would tire of them after a short duration. The only positive that emerged was the self discovery that she was a quick learner and developing skills to meet the situation came easily. That would come in handy wherever life's trip took her.

Whenever she looked back on her life she did not like what she saw. Robbed of a normal childhood by a father that ran away with another woman when she was five, and a mother who then paid little attention to her as she wallowed in self pity. Friendships were hard to make and more difficult to keep. She was too serious for playmates who just wanted to have fun. In high school she was not interested in boys, clothes, or loud music, so few other girls made overtures of companionship. She did not begrudge any of this. That was the way it was. That is who she was and still is.

She should probably get a place of her own to live in, but she felt sorry for her mother and there had been a growing dependency on Mac over the years. She was not sure if her mother could make it without her being there. Dependency is a destroyer of initiative and action. Having a conscience sure gets in the way of decisions.

Mac recognized that in Tommy there was a myriad of good opportunities. A ground level chance to be involved in something new that peaked her interest was the greatest outlook. She could also picture him as a father figure through whom she could learn much about life and people. She did not know too many older people but figured for sure that the wisdom she sought comes with life experiences. She was ready for new travels in knowing and doing.

Because of her looks and shape men often showed attention to her. There was no encouragement on her part, and a stern rebuff was most effective. Men were not paying mind to her for conversation, and that brought about a certain hostility. At some point that might change, and she knew that if she ever wanted to have children the biological clock was ticking on mercilessly. Yet, she was focusing on the here and now. There was the sense that Tommy would be able to guide her through all of the segments of life in a proper and satisfactory way. More than anything else he represented the feature in her life most lacking of that of having someone to talk to, to confide in. Maybe then she could figure out why she was so different from other people. Maybe then she could be proud of that fact rather than merely accepting it.

FIVE

A week later the desk and chair were ensconced in the office. Some desk accessories and an additional phone line to the desk and the work space was fully operational. Mac stopped in each day to check on the progress. When all was ready, she started her afternoon quest.

The first time she settled at the desk, she exclaimed as if she were a little girl, "Let the fun begin."

"You better tell yourself twiddling your thumbs is fun. That's all there is right now. In fact, to keep myself busy besides reading I am making a list of the things that are harder for me to do now than some years back."

"Like chasing young women?"

"That goes too far back. More like this morning before I got dressed I tried to clip my toe nails. Just bending over was difficult, and what probably would be a thirty second task took me ten minutes."

"I'm glad I had lunch already. Picturing an old man doing his toe nails would have daunted my appetite."

"Mine, too. I skipped breakfast. Almost forgot to clean my dentures. My best advice to you is not to grow old. Adversities and adversaries come in bunches, often unanticipated and most often unwelcome."

"I will definitely keep that in mind, although until you reveal the secret of how to stop the hands of time, I suspect old age will get the better of me. In the meantime, try to be positive, boss."

She looked fetching in a red sweater and short plaid skirt. He was not too old to appreciate what he could look at. "And by the way, don't forget who is the boss."

She smiled. "If I do forget, I am sure you will remind me."

As if by magic, the heretofore dead telephone sprang to life. Mac answered it on the third ring. "Good afternoon, this is the Thomas Lloyd Detective Agency. How can we help you?"

Tom listened intently. His eyebrows, scraggly as they might be, were raised at what he heard. Mac's voice was emphatic. "I am sorry we are booked today. There is an open appointment tomorrow at 2:30." Silence for a moment. "That will be fine. Name please." Another period of silence. "Can you spell that, please." Another pause. "That will be fine, Mr. Klerature. We will see you tomorrow at 2:30." She turned to Tom. "See, business is booming already."

"Why did you put him off until tomorrow?"

"I wanted him to think we are busy. A psychological advantage."

"Clever, but dangerous. I will have to watch you every minute."

"You will like what you see."

"I already do. I also want to like what I hear."

"I also want to learn from you, not just about this undertaking but all about life. Everything there is from toe nails to toe holds. Above and below as well as sideways."

"You may be disappointed. I am just an ordinary old man."

"A national treasure in my view. If I can absorb your life experience while I am still young, the way I look at it I will age to perfection."

"Maybe you can reciprocate and infuse me with your youthful vitality."

She seemed overly serious at his attempt at humor. "If only things could work that way, there might be a better venture than a detective agency."

He walked over to her and leaned on the desk. "Let's just see how it all plays out. One gem of philosophy that I have tried to live by all of my life is that if you don't have great expectations you don't have big disappointments."

She smiled again and patted his hand. "I think I will start a journal of gems of wisdom so I can keep count as you spout forth."

"Might wind up to be a very slim volume."

"Might exceed War and Peace."

"We'll see."

"Most definitely."

SIX

Mac arrived at 1:45, and it was then just a waiting game until 2:30 rolled around. Mr. Klerature did not show up until close to 3:00. He was, if one were to affix on such a notion, a typical senior. He was short, and had rounded shoulders and thinning gray hair. Walking was more of a shuffling of feet as if each step needed to be planned in advance. "Sorry I'm late," he announced in a scratchy and weak voice. "Traffic is bad today."

Mac greeted him in an upbeat manner. "Welcome, sir."

Tom moved to the entrance where Mr. Klerature lingered just inside the door. He shook the man's hand firmly. "I am Tom Lloyd. Come and sit a spell and we'll see what we can do for you."

The man sat in the chair in front of Tom's desk. Mac pulled her chair close by and opened a notebook so she could take notes.

Tom thought it best to make some light conversation in the event the client was nervous or apprehensive about being there. "Before we discuss anything or you fill out our client form, tell me something about yourself."

The man fidgeted in the chair. His voice shook perceptively. "Not much to tell. I was an accountant in my former life in Chicago. My wife died seven years ago. I retired and moved down here to Sunset Acres to be close to my daughter." A pause that appeared painful. "I shouldn't have done that."

Silence prompted Tom to inquire, "Why not?"

"Oh, it has been a series of heartaches and disappointments."

Another period of silence. "Don't feel you have to talk about it."

"She has just gotten her third divorce. She is bitter and combative, and couldn't care less that I am here. But, that is not why I need your help."

"I'm listening," Tom offered.

"It is my granddaughter that I am concerned about. She is twenty-two, been sheltered and ignored her entire life, and naive to the hilt. She especially has little social skills and as far as I can tell no experience with men. Out of the blue, this older man, I would say in his forties, has shown a great interest in her. He has swept her off her feet, lavishing her with attention and gifts, and alluring promises. She is a plain Jane, if you know what I mean. So, I don't know what is going on or why. I would like to find out for sure and for you to check this fellow out."

Tom leaned back in his chair. "I can do that, but won't know what is involved until I get in to it. It might turn out to be expensive."

"Like what?"

"There would be a $500 retainer, and then $75 and hour plus expenses."

The man was pensive for a moment. "Worth it, I guess, for my peace of mind and to prevent her from making a mistake and getting hurt. I just have a bad feeling about this guy."

"Alright then." Tom reached in to a desk drawer and pulled out some papers. "Fill this client form out. Then you can give me the names, addresses of this guy and your granddaughter, as well as a $500 check, and I'll get started right away. I will report to you what I find as I go along, and you can end it when you think you know enough to do what you think you should do."

An hour later, Mr. Klerature was gone. Mac moved over to

Tom's desk. "What now, boss?"

"First, we deposit the check. It is probably good, but that is the first step. Second, you start a log to keep track of time and expenses. Do you have a computer?"

"No."

"I'll get you one so you can keep it electronically. Easier and more efficient. I will teach you all about it. Then, we will search the public records to find out as much as we can on this Bruce Higgins fellow that way. If that does not produce enough to raise a red flag we will have to be more active."

Mac smiled broadly. "Exciting already."

"If you like drudgery, you will be excited."

"What do you think about Mr. Klerature?"

"Too early for a good assessment. However, chances are he is not telling us all he knows or all that motivates him here. Human nature tends towards secretive and elusive sentiments."

"Another pearl of wisdom."

"Not wisdom as much as caution is as caution does."

"There you go again."

"Do you want to be a detective or a student?"

"Can't I be both?"

"Normally, I would say no, but in your case it is probably going to happen anyway."

"I second that."

SEVEN

The next day, just as Tom was about to show Mac how to do a public records search for Bruce Higgins, the telephone rang and Mac made an appointment the following afternoon for a potential client. Her smile said it all.

There were a number of Bruce Higgins that showed up in the search, although none of them seemed to be the person of their interest. Even the Department of Motor Vehicles did not show a car registered to him. Tom theorized that he might have a business and the car might be registered to the business. It still was strange in this day and age that the computer revealed nothing about him. Tom wondered that Bruce Higgins might not be his real name.

"So," Mac noted with a degree of exasperation, "What now, Tommy?"

"Ah, lass, you need patience as we pursue other avenues. If you want to be a detective without patience you will experience long periods of tedium and boredom."

"What avenues?"

"He lives in a town house. We'll drive over there and copy the license plate number off the car parked in front. If that isn't enough, you wanted to do surveillance, so we'll wait some morning and follow him when he leaves."

"Now you are talking."

"No, there won't be much talking. And, my child, you will

see how truly boring detective work can be. It might be hours, and it might be a day for some reason he does not leave his house. We might get lucky; we might not."

"I'm with you."

"Yes, you are. It will be awhile before I send you out on your own. I don't want to have to worry about you."

"I think you just like being with me."

He smiled. "That, too."

The next afternoon, the potential client came in. Adele Scheinfeld was, in some ways, a shocking older female figure. She was visibly in poor health, and it was obvious the aging process had not been kind to her. There are some elderly women one can easily guess were beauties in their youth. Adele was not one of them.

Mac greeted her and showed her to the chair in front of Tom's desk. Tom smiled and tried to put his friendliest foot forward. "I don't know if you are a Miss or a Mrs, so I will address you as Adele. I am Thomas Lloyd. Just call me Tom. Alright?"

There was a warm smile through cracked lips. Her voice was stronger than her body predicted. "O.K., Tom Alright."

He chuckled. "I love it when my contemporaries are spunky."

"Spunky may be all I have left."

"I doubt that, but it covers a multiple of sins."

"You seem robust."

"Fortunately, I enjoy good health."

"Not me. I'm a haggard old lady. The product of an unhappy and strained life, and now a walking medical text book."

He figured he better change the subject. The one thing he did learn from his disinterested neighbors at the retirement community was that talking about health issues is a Pandora's box. The spigot is difficult to turn off. "Why would you, at this point, need a private detective?"

"I don't need a detective."

He was taken aback. Mac's eyes widened. "So, why are you here?"

"By your advertisement you are a senior, and I need a strong senior man to act as my companion, a bodyguard of sorts."

Mac's eyebrows raised. Tom cleared his throat thinking back on his recent comic idea of having a senior escort service. "That's not what I do."

"You seem strong and able, so please hear me out before you throw me out."

"Most definitely."

She squirmed noticeably in the chair. "I really don't know where else to go or what else to do. I am hoping you will help me."

Tom liked this woman and already felt sorry for her. If he could, he would help her, but he did not see it in the cards. "I can listen. Maybe, nothing more."

She took what appeared to be a deep breath, although it might have been a painful sigh. "I married late in life as no man was interested in me. I was, I know very well, an ugly duckling and still am. An admission of obviousness is an understatement. Anyway, he had money and influence. He did not love me. I knew that and was prepared to accept that. To this day I still do not know why he married me. While he never hit me, he was mean and condescending most of the time. Emotional wounds are as painful as physical ones. We adopted a teenage girl, Ellie, and she became my life. She was smart and talented, and appreciated my caring and nurturing. Her father was luke warm towards her, although I think he tried in his own way to be a father. Without any explanation one day he left us for another woman, one I think he was seeing before me and all along during the marriage." Tom noted the frown on Mac's face. "I got a divorce and full custody of Ellie. He had to support her until she turned twenty-one and had to pay her full college tuition. He had to pay me alimony until he died, I died or remarried. He has made it clear of his intolerance for these payments all of these years, and an intolerance that has, as far as I can tell, developed to a full animosity and annoyance with me. I have often thought that he wants to arrange an accident for me."

Adele stopped speaking and her clouded eyes gazed off in the distance. "Would you like some water?" Mac offered.

"No, thanks, dear. It is just hard at times to express what has just been in thoughts. Well, anyway, Ellie is a teacher, married, and has three children. She lives and teaches in Charleston, South Carolina. One of the children, a daughter, Candice, is getting married in a month. It is going to be a big wedding at one of the plantations there. Naturally, I am invited. Ellie has invited her father also. While she has not had much to do with him over the years, she thinks this may mend fences. I am afraid to face him alone."

Her silence prompted Tom to speak. "Have you tried to explain to Ellie how you feel? Maybe, she can disinvite him?"

It was an awkward moment before she responded. "She knows how I feel, and she has no love for him. Yet, she is such an idealistic person, such a pure soul, that she feels that if she gives him this chance a good side of him will emerge. I don't agree with her, but cannot and will not force her to do otherwise."

"How come you are not living with Ellie?"

"Small house and tight finances. My cousin, Florence, owns the nursing home I am in so I get special arrangements from her. Candice is marrying into money. That is why the wedding will be so lavish."

"Have you considered not going to the wedding?"

"Yes, but it is so important to Ellie that I be there. I just can't disappoint her. Candice also has a special place in my heart. I am in the proverbial position between a rock and a hard place."

"What about going with your cousin? I assume she has also

been invited."

"She has but is unable to free herself up to go."

"Perhaps, she can arrange for someone to accompany you."

"She really does not know anything about all of this. Frankly, I would be too embarrassed to ask her."

"I am not saying I will do it, but if I do it such will be quite expensive. There is a $500 retainer; $75 an hour, although I might make it a flat daily rate, and all expenses. Can you handle that?"

"Each monthly alimony payment as well as my Social Security goes to the nursing home. I have some savings from the earlier years. I have to do what has to be done."

"My Assistant, Mac here, keeps a journal of what she terms my wise sayings. I am sure she will add some of the statements you have made here."

Mac nodded. Adele looked at the young woman with added appreciation. "At times, years are not borders."

Mac smiled. "Nor should they be."

Tom pulled out a client form from the desk. "Adele, please fill this out. I need to think about this, and I will let you know by tomorrow one way or the other." He shook her small hand, her grasp firmer than he expected.

Adele hugged Mac before she left. Mac looked out of the window until Adele drove off. "I am surprised she is able to drive."

Tom chuckled. "I think that little old lady could surprise both of us. Some powers are well hidden."

Mac returned to her desk. "I have to write that one down, too. Well, boss, what are you going to do?"

"Not sure yet. I better talk it over with my wife. She may not be too keen on such an undertaking. What do you think?"

"My take of the money would be good, but you need to decide this on your own. Probably, could be argued both ways."

EIGHT

"I don't know if you are just plain dumb or crazy," April yelled in a loud voice as he finished relating Adele's office visit. "Maybe, both," she added in a tone bordering on nasty.

Tom wanted to keep his tone soft hoping it would have a calming effect. "You know I have always had a disposition to help people. That is why I became a lawyer and why I have started this business. There is often no way to predict what shape or form that need may take. I must be flexible. Try to be understanding."

April's voice lowered as she took a deep breath. "I try Tom, really I do. I am just at my limit. We have been together for a long time, and I do love you, but I just can't live with your restless spirit any longer. It affects my well being if not my sanity. We are at the stage of our lives when we should be enjoying the fruits of our harvest and not starting to plant the crops. I just want to relax, enjoy peace and quiet, and not be concerned about the problems of strangers. Is that too much to ask for?"

He tried to hug her but she pushed him away. "No, it is not too much to ask for. But, I am not wanting that. I admit I have a restless spirit but it is more than that. There are many cries for help in the wilderness and a dwindling number of people who hear those cries and are willing to help. Please try and understand and be patient with me. These are things I feel I must do as long as I am able to."

"No, Tom, I don't understand and, frankly, I don't want to

understand it. We are on different roads. You will do what you feel you must do. I know that, but I am finished accepting it."

He noted the tears swelling up in her eyes. He could not remember the last time he saw her cry. He felt badly, and he could even see from her perspective she was right. They had become two completely different people and if they had just met there there would have been no sense of compatibility. "April, I do not want to make you unhappy. What do you suggest?"

"Let's try living apart for awhile. If you come to your senses, we can try again. If not, and of course the children will never accept it or understand it, we must go our separate ways."

Tom was perceptive enough to know that this was not a spur of the moment thought on her part. It had probably been brewing for some time. It is just that this incident brought it to the surface. He also realized that the impetus for the development was not merely relating Adele's visit but the underlying decision that he had already made but had not confronted that he was going to take on that assignment. "April, are you sure there is no other way?"

She looked out of the window to a distant view that she had undoubtedly studied before. Her voice was hushed and barely audible. "I am sure."

He recalled seeing rental apartments behind the shopping center where the office was. "I'll find a place and move out. Although I wish you would reconsider this decision. It will really not simplify either of our lives. And, as you say, the children will not understand it. You will have to explain it to them. I know how and why you feel this way, but it is not convincing in the telling."

NINE

"Well, Tommy, what have you decided?" Mac had just entered the office when she shot out the question. "I couldn't sleep last night wondering what you will do."

For an instant he closed his eyes. "I am going to do it."

"I would have bet that you would."

"But, that is not the only upheaval."

"Ah, so?"

"My wife has asked me to move out."

"Wow!"

"This was just the straw that broke the camel's back. She has been unhappy with who I am and what I do."

Mac slumped in the chair before his desk. "You don't have to give me any details or explanations."

"I know. Since you now have left the florist to be here full time I don't want to have any secrets from you. If I talk about it, perhaps I can more readily accept it. Marriage is basically a series of compromises. It is usually not a problem to compromise about the minor things, and if there are children compromise is a necessity. In some major aspects compromise would be a surrender. She thinks I can change who I am. Perhaps so, if I really wanted to. Yet, it is more complex than that. A long time ago I had an experience that taught me that to be honest with others I must first be honest with myself, even at the risk of losing a friend or other value. My parents had some dear friends who also had a boy of my age. Naturally, we did many things together and became best friends. When in high school, there were two girls our age who were in the same circle of friends. I still remember their names, which when I think about it is revealing in itself. They were Marilyn and Audrey. My friend confided in me that he was in love with Marilyn. Secretly, I was also crazy about Marilyn, but because he professed such strong feelings towards her and since I did not want to jeopardize the friendship, I said my romantic feelings were for Audrey. We made it known to them, and they said they both were in love with the same one of us. They would not say which one. I know you can guess what happened next?"

Mac reached for his hand that was stretched out on the desk. "It is obvious, but you need to finish."

"Well, we kept pressing them and finally they admitted it was me they preferred. I pined in secret for Marilyn. I really couldn't bring myself to get close to Audrey, and the girls eventually lost complete interest in us. My friend said it all did not matter to him, but I knew it did. Nothing was the same after that. It was not an easy lesson for a youngster to absorb, but the significance has always lurked in my mind."

Mac came around the desk and hugged him. "Tommy, you are only human. I wish I had as few weaknesses as you have. I kick myself so often I am black and blue."

"Trying to make the old man feel better?"

"Is it working?"

"You may want to write this down. A regret dominates the soul. Who could not feel better in the presence of a high-spirited assistant?"

"My job is multifaceted, I can see that."

"I am going to call Adele, and then we will drive over to Bruce Higgins' house to see if there is a car parked in the front. I'll bring you back to the office and then go over to the rental office behind the office and seal my fate."

TEN

There were no cars parked at the front of Higgins' townhouse. Tom wrote down the license plate numbers of the closest parked cars just in case.

There is much to say for being at the right place at the right time. At the rental office of the Belaire Apartments, they had just released for rental one of the furnished models as they were approaching full occupancy. It was a one-bedroom apartment, completely furnished right down to dishes, pots, and silverware. The only things Tom would have to bring would be sheets, towels, and his clothing. He went to the department store and bought some sheets and towels, and then went home and packed the car with his clothing. April was out, so that avoided an awkward meeting. He left her a note, once again apologizing and telling her where he would be and to contact him if she should need anything. He reiterated that he was who he was and that he had strong commitments to himself as well as to her. He would gladly come back if she had a change of mind and heart. He closed by saying that he loved her.

Back at the office, he filled Mac in on developments. He also planned to go back to the Higgins' home that night to check on any car parked there. She offered to go with him, but he told her to get her rest instead. There might be other things for her to do if this idea did not reach fruition.

Just before midnight, he drove past the Higgins' house. A black

Lexus was parked there. He wrote down the plate number and hoped this would lead to some critical information. The next day they ran the plate number, and it came back as a Jessie Holder at that address. Since they did not know what Higgins looked like, the picture on the driver's license would have to await Mr Klerature's inspection. In the meantime, just in the event they had hit pay dirt, they did a background check on Jessie Holder. That proved most revealing. Jessie Holder had served two prison terms for fraud.

When Tom returned from getting the plate number, it was no surprise to him that the first night in the apartment and in a new bed that he should have a series of interesting dreams. Two female figures dominated scenes as they unfolded. As close as he could figure it out, Mac represented compassion and Adele ushered forth adventure. Would symbols be the driving force of his future?

In the morning, he related the dreams to Mac. Her look was serious. "I find it fascinating that you dream of me. I have had dreams involving you, but they are more than dreams. I have not had a father, a bit like Ellie, and no other male figure has emerged in my life or that I have had a feeling for him and a desire for me to know him and understand him until I met you. Tommy, I am making you my official mentor."

He smiled. "I am honored, but as I told you before I sense you will be doing more for me than I will do for you. Since my own children are now geographically and emotionally far removed from me, I am making you my adopted daughter."

"I don't know how you may feel about this, but I want you to teach me about all sorts of things, about life."

"That is a tall order. I am not sure I am qualified."

"From what I feel and have already observed, you are super qualified."

He came up to her and hugged her warmly. "I will try and hope you will not be disappointed."

"I doubt I will be. I want you to teach me how to love so that if the right man comes along I will recognize it and be able to do something about it."

"Perhaps, that is something we can learn together. I am not sure I know the true depth and strength of love. When I met April, we had so much in common and she seemed so interested in me and having a future together, Hollywood images transported my mind to thinking this must be love. As life itself is multifaceted and multidimensional, love has many functions, many faces so to speak. It can be different things in various situations and with different people. Above all else, I see now you can only get out of it what you put into it."

"Wow! A tough thought to understand. How can I ever live it?"

"Like with most other things, a little at a time. Trial and error, and with any failure serving as reinforcement for what you seek. The most important thought, take each day one at a time. Each day is a journey to tomorrow."

"Will you hold my hand along the way?"

"Not only that, I'll pick up the pieces and help you construct what love is in store for you. And, just maybe, along the way I will find some answers for me as well."

Another comforting hug served as a bond and an impetus for things to come. The unknown is significant at any age.

ELEVEN

Mr. Klerature telephoned to tell them that Jessie Holder and Bruce Higgins were one in the same, and his granddaughter was shocked and disappointed but grateful for his intervention. He said he would come in that afternoon to pay the final bill. Mac was eager to get her 25% since she had no income since leaving the florist.

Adele telephoned and said she had made airline and hotel reservations for the weekend of the wedding, as well as having Florence mail in the initial fee check as she did not have her own account. They would be flying to Charleston that Thursday morning, and on Friday there would be a rehearsal and a family dinner at the hotel. The wedding was Saturday afternoon in the gardens of the plantation with the reception following at the main house at the plantation. Ellie had arranged for transportation for them by limousine. Adele asked him if it was agreeable that she booked adjoining rooms at the hotel. He joked by telling her that if she wanted to save some money she could just reserve one room with two beds. At their age the usual protocol was unnecessary.

A week passed and Tom telephoned April to see how she was doing. She was cordial although distant, and was frank to admit that she was comfortable with his absence. He refrained from commenting that he too was not upset with the new arrangement. When he thought about it, he was actually at a new peace with himself. He refrained from saying he loved her when he said goodbye, and afterward he was glad he did not say it. He fully realized that the long-standing comfort of their being together was not truly love. He had not thought about it in those terms, but it lingered in his mind as something he probably should have faced long ago. He wondered how many other married couples merely accept comfort and habit as love. Perhaps, she knew that as well. Were all of those years wasted? The harshest realization an old person might make is that the life lived has been wasted. Undoubtedly, he would dwell upon this further in some quiet moments.

Two new cases came in. One was from the lady who owned the florist next door, Mac's former employer, who hired them to track down a customer who refused to pay for a rather large floral arrangement and then disappeared. The other was from a retiree who had become enticed by an investment proposal for a resort to be built in the Grand Cayman Islands. He had taken advantage of a free trip there to see the proposed site and was duly impressed. Before shelling out any money, he wanted Tom to check on the investment company and to contact some of the other investors for their legitimacy. That might take some digging and would keep Mac busy with the computer.

As busy and involved Tom and Mac might get, the two made time to exchange pleasantries and probing thoughts. As Tom had thought at times that his philosophy against the stream of convention made him one for the ages, an expansion was now in order to make that two for the ages. Perhaps, she was meant to be his alter ego. Mac would go out and get them lunch to share at the office along with their conversation. She also insisted on going with him at the end of the day to the apartment to make him a light dinner, usually a salad, before she went on to her mother.

An interesting result of sustained concentrated conversation is an acute recollection of one's past that may have been pushed to the background in the rush of every day life. Mac was eager to hear of his early life, and in relating incidents he further recalled other events that he had long since forgotten. One, which was a classic case of poetic justice, occurred shortly after the Marilyn-Audrey fiasco. He had developed a strong crush on Rhona King, a studious beauty that was active in many student activities. She not only rebuked his advances she lectured him on his inane behavior, his lack of dignity and finesse, as well as his boring demeanor. That put him in a low place and it was a long and painful period before his esteem was built back up. A lesson that he could convey to Mac was that there might be a deeper meaning to the saying of not counting your chickens before they hatch.

None of us is perfect, but that is no excuse for acts of unkindness to others. Especially is this the case when it ripens into a regret. While he told Mac that dwelling on regrets is counterproductive and is a subtle way of torturing the soul, he did have a deep regret of an unkindness he bestowed on another. Just as Rhona King could have merely told him that she already had a boyfriend or simply was not interested in him without spelling out a litany of his weaknesses, an incident occurred in his past of which he was particularly unhappy about. In his early days at the law firm, he was given a new personal secretary, Linda Avery. While he did not know the details of her background, he was aware that she was a struggling single mother. She was a pleasant person but not very efficient. She often made repeated mistakes and was slow in anticipating his work needs. She was trying her best, and in time he probably could have guided her to a satisfactory end, but in a bout of intolerance he had her fired without notice. The lesson he learned from that, and which he wanted Mac to digest, was that it often takes more effort to be unkind and is not worthy of human behavior. A host of good deeds and worthwhile moments can be obscured by an act of poor judgment. Harsh moments can haunt you forever. It is a noble stance to be proud in the development of your life. As George Bernard Shaw ably phrased it – Life is not about finding yourself. Life is about creating yourself.

Mac was quick to relate that she could not recall any events she wished she could relive, although there were times in which she could have handled a situation and the people involved in it better. Her main accomplishment was looking after her mother, and even in that she might actually be doing her a disservice. She was becoming more convinced that she was the cause of her mother's dependency on her and that if she was left to fend for herself she might do just fine. Of course, that too would free her up to live the life Tommy was showing her to be out there.

TWELVE

There probably would have been enough time on the plane and at the hotel for them to know each other better, but Tom thought it might be of use if he met with Adele for lunch prior to the trip. She was receptive to the idea, offering a quip that she would probably be billed for the lunch as part of his services. He thought that was a good idea and told her so. Her response was sincere, "I have always had a big mouth."

He picked her up at the nursing home and took her to an Italian restaurant he liked. She was frank to admit that it had been a long time since she dined out, and longer yet taken out by a man. It wound up to be a treat for her. It was even a bigger treat for him. Her conversation was intelligent and witty, and it did not take long for him to look beyond her plain looks and sickly presence to discover a person with a probing mind and a charming and warm demeanor. In fact, as he described her to Mac after he was back at the office, she was a secret treasure, a prize package. Mac's eyebrows raised as she thought to herself, "This is going to be one interesting trip for the two seniors."

In the car on the way to the restaurant, Tom was thinking, "What shall I say to break the ice?"

As if she heard his thought, she blurted out, "Does your billing start when you picked me up or when we get to the restaurant?"

He chuckled. "Dear lady, the meter is not running. You will

probably bill me for being my lunch partner."

It was not perfume he smelled, rather it was the soap residue in her thinning gray hair, and he had to admit to himself that despite popular concepts to the contrary old can be fresh and alluring. He had come across some sayings about old people in all that reading he did awaiting clients. Two came to mind befitting the occasion.

Beautiful young people are accidents of nature, but beautiful old people are works of art.
- Eleanor Roosevelt

Some people, no matter how old they get, never lose their beauty –they merely move it from their faces to their hearts.

- Martin Buxbaum

It may be true that one cannot fully know and appreciate being old until one is actually old, and it also may be true that being old does not diminish the force and desire to live life to its fullest. That was true for Tom, and he liked to think that it very well might be true for Adele.

They discovered they liked the same Italian dish, and ordered two portions of eggplant parmigiano. "My dentures are no barrier to appreciating this dish," Tom said lightheartedly.

"I still have my own teeth, probably the only part of me still intact and original. I use them more for attempting to block what my tongue wants to say than for eating or smiling. Maybe, that is why I still have my teeth. Not much ever to smile about."

"Not even in succeeding in getting a private detective to not only protect you but to let that louse see you now have men falling at your feet."

There came a smile, albeit a small one. "If that did happen, I would trip over them before I realized they were there."

The food arrived, and for several moments they ate in a relaxed mode. "You are hard on yourself, dear lady. You probably think you deserve that. I don't see it that way."

She took off her glasses and handed them to him. "You need to try these. I see me as others see me."

"That is your mistake. You need to see yourself as you see you."

"One in the same," and her voice trailed off.

"Then you need to take a new and fresh look. I see plenty of life and vigor in you."

She took her glasses back and put them on. "Maybe, I should get rose-colored lenses put in. I would love to have a positive attitude."

"Now you are talking. Being old is not the end of the road. It is just a resting place. The best part of the journey lays ahead."

"If I focus on Ellie and Candice there is incentive to move on. Otherwise, death will be my savior."

"None of that talk with me. You have plenty of living to do, plenty of scenic overlooks to bask in emotional sustenance."

"I doubt such exists."

"Anything is possible for the mind to see."

"Are you sure you are an old man?"

"An old man who is glad he isn't young, too much agitation and uncertainty. We do not have to be old on the inside."

She was silent for a moment. He saw the tear roll down her wrinkled cheek as the thin shoulders slumped and she lay her fork down. "I am afraid it is too late for me."

He could tell he had much to do to show this woman that her life was far from over, pleasures not so distant as to be unattainable.

"Ellie would not like to hear that kind of talk. Neither do I."

"Ellie calls me every day. She is the reason I am still living, but living is a far cry from being alive."

"You stick with me, kid, and you will not need rose-colored lenses. You will discover you are very much alive and kicking."

She only finished a small part of her meal and took the boxed remainder back to the home. She thanked him when they pulled up to the door. "No, dear lady, thank you. Your company made my day enjoyable and memorable. I hope I did the same for you."

A broader smile this time. "You did. You very much did."

THIRTEEN

The next day Tom had flowers from the shop next door sent to Adele. The note read: *The essence of the budding of your future reveals a beautiful flower. I await to see the full blossom.* Upon receipt, she telephoned him and thanked him profusely. "I only receive flowers from Ellie on my birthday. To receive these was a delightful surprise. I suppose you are expecting a bonus?"

"My bonus," he responded in earnest, "Will be seeing the blossoming in all of its splendor."

"Do other old men say such things in a similar cockeyed way?"

"Don't know. I can't and won't speak for others. Besides, you are my secret."

"Swell, then, the jury is in. You are one crazy old man, but I accept such irrational behavior."

When he hung up, Mac chimed in, "I believe it is against private investigator ethics to romance a client."

"Not romancing, just supplying full service."

"Anyway, I have first dibs on you."

"You are first in line, for sure."

"That is just the place I want to be."

"I have another surprise for you. I am sending in the application for you to be a licensed sleuth. Here it is. I filled it in as best as I could. Complete it, sign it, and with my check off it goes. I also have a box here of business cards printed for you."

She came over to hug him. "You are one sweet old man."

"Sweet begets sweet."

"Another one to write down."

"Words to live by."

"I have an idea I want to run by you."

"Fire away."

"You know the situation with my mother. Could I stay in the apartment while you are running away with Adele? I will be able to see if she can get along without me."

"Sure. No problem. In fact, I think it is a good plan. I even have an extra key to give you."

"If it works out, and assuming the fees keep coming in, I can get my own place so when Mr. Right comes along I will have a place to entertain him."

"You are just chock full of good ideas, except you know I will chaperone any entertaining sessions."

"That is a given. Your influence rubs off on me with it all."

They then reviewed progress being made on the two other cases they had. The florist owner was well aware that their fee might be greater than any recovery eventually obtained but she still wanted to pursue it as a matter of principle. The buyer seemed to have totally disappeared, and maybe the only way to get a lead on his whereabouts would be to talk to the folks at the funeral home as the flowers were delivered there for a funeral. As to the Cayman Islands venture, Mac had compiled an extensive list of purported investors although there did not appear to be much on the investment company itself. Apparently, it had been formed recently for the sole purpose of this investment scheme.

A few days later, Mac's license arrived. She shouted with excitement and hugged him again. The hugs were warm and sincere, and he appreciated each one. "Now, lass, you have the credentials, so

I am going to let you go to the funeral home on your own. Find out which funeral the flowers were delivered for, the family involved and contact information, and anything else they might know that could be helpful."

She was keyed up. "Count on me, boss."

R. Nathan and Sons was one of the oldest and largest funeral homes in the area. It probably was one of the busiest as well. Every time Tom drove by the place by the way the parking lot was full there must have been a funeral going on. Very clever to have such a business in an area with so many old folks nearby.

Mac had not been fully aware of such a place. Now, as she drove in the entrance she admired the finely landscaped grounds and the inviting appeal of the white stucco building with a hint of Spanish design, as well as the towering palm trees surrounding it. She had read once about how expensive funerals were, and although she had not discussed it with her mother she duly expected to have her cremated when the time came.

The parking lot was empty, so it was probably a good time to ask questions. She felt confident as she was on a mission and so much appreciated Tommy having such trust in her to send her out on her own. She would never want to disappoint him. That is the kind of bond she felt with him, probably the closest thing to love that she had ever felt. He had said there are different kinds of love, and since she looked to him as a father it is most likely the kind of love that a daughter feels towards a father. The feelings she had for her mother were more akin to care and concern which is probably an aspect of love, although she was sure she did not love her mother. She would not like to think that feeling sorry for a person is love.

Mac pushed open the large oak door to the vestibule. There was nobody around. She walked to the back and said aloud, "Hello. Anyone here?"

It was a moment before a young man emerged from the back. He was dressed in a brown suit and had a floral tie on. He was tall, taller than Tommy. "May I help you?" his voice was deep and diction clear.

She figured he was one of the R. Nathan sons. "Sure enough," as she handed him one of her cards.

"Want to arrange a funeral for a client?"

She smiled, noticing him looking over her body in the clinging dress she was wearing. "No, and not mine either."

He smiled broadly, a nice and inviting smile. "Then what brings you here?"

"Are you the owner?"

"Sort of."

"What does that mean?"

"I am Andrew Nathan, the son of one of R. Nathan's sons, his grandson."

"Is your father or grandfather around?"

"My grandfather passed some twenty year ago, and my father is retired. My sister and I run the business."

"Good. I am trying to locate the family that held a funeral here on May 14."

"Why don't you wait here. I'll go back and check the books."

"Fine. Thank you."

"No problem," as he smiled again. Her eyes wandered to his left hand. No wedding ring. Thanks to Tommy she had a new found interest, perhaps better to phrase it a curiosity, in men.

Some five minutes later he returned. He handed her a slip of paper. "Just one funeral that day. Albert Hornstein. Arrangements were made by his daughter, Monica Thorpe. Her telephone number is on the paper."

"One more question. Do you keep a list of flower deliveries for each funeral?"

"Sure. The family is interested in who sent flowers so they can send a thank you later on. We turn the list over to them."

"Do you retain any of the information?"

"Just the name of the florist. You do ask a lot of questions. Why is it so important?"

"We are trying to locate a deadbeat for a florist."

"Oh. Aren't you awfully young to be a detective?"

"Now who is asking many questions. If you must know, it is my natural inclination. Aren't you too young to be an undertaker?"

"It's in my genes. The one drawback is that I don't get enough chances to meet pretty young women who are not grieving."

She smiled. "Then that is an undertaking that an undertaker has to work on."

He looked at her left hand, observing there was no ring. "I am right now."

"That is obvious. Do you keep a guest list of those who attend the funeral?"

"There is a guest book for those who care to sign it. That, too, is turned over to the family." A pause that Mac liked to describe as dramatic. "How did you get the name Mac? Were your parents expecting a boy?"

"My name is Michelle. As a child I only wanted to eat macaroni and cheese so everyone started to call me Mac. It stuck, and I like it better than Michelle."

"Are you married?"

"No."

"Engaged?"

"No."

"Boy friend?"

"No. And you?"

"None of the above." Another dramatic pause. "Can I call you sometime?"

"You have my card. Thank you for your help."

"My pleasure."

She turned to leave, thinking to herself, "No, my pleasure."

FOURTEEN

Even for Tom, it was an unusual dream. Instead of an elongated episode that reflected or resembled an aspect of his life, this dream was a series of snippets of where he had been and what he had done. There were fragments from his childhood, the school years, and later on as if they were blocks building on each other. There were the insurance company, the law firm, and the detective agency. The major female players emerged as they were, as they are, or as he imagined them to be. In a series of mind shots there were Marilyn, Audrey, Linda, Rhona, Mac, and Adele. April and the children weaved in and out. A rainbow would appear in between many of the snap shots. Rainbows had always held a special appeal for him from the time as a boy when he saw his first one. It became a world of wonderment that opened before him. That sensation was enhanced the first time, and each time since, when he heard Judy Garland sing Somewhere Over the Rainbow. Behind the fleeting image of Mac there was a double rainbow.

The dream was as if the proverbial flashes of his life appearing before his eyes that they say happens when you are about to die. So much so that he awoke sweating. He had rarely thought about his own death, although for every elderly person it lurks in the shadows. As he sat in the bed, it came to him that what would bother him most would not be death itself but leaving things unfinished. At this juncture there seemed so much remaining to be accomplished, to see how things in the works would turn out. April had said it was too late in life to plant seeds. He did not buy into that. It was never too late to start things anew. It would be best if the completed picture came to view so that one might be satisfied that the effort was worth it. Life can be looked at not just as one endeavor but rather as a continuum of lives, each separate and yet joined together by commonality.

In the morning, he described the dream to Mac. Her usual perky demeanor changed to a look of sadness. "Don't you ever die on me, mister. I need you every step of the way. If you die I will never speak to you again."

"Hey, it was just a dream. There's lots of life in the ole boy yet. Plus, I have too many women in my life that I cannot disappoint."

"Keep telling yourself that."

"I know you will keep on reminding me."

"You bet! That's an assistant's job."

"Maybe, I am not paying you enough."

"I like the sound of that."

"What do you think the meaning is of a double rainbow behind you in the dream?"

She thought for a moment. "Has to be that we are a matching set. More alike than anything else, each spectacular apart and together."

"Sounds reasonable. You heard of the saying when a person is unique One for the Ages. Perhaps, we are Two for the Ages."

"I also like the sound of that."

A real mystery developed. Mac telephoned Monica Thorpe, daughter of the man for whom the funeral was held. She had the list of who had sent flowers, and sent a thank you note to those who had addresses. Not only was there no address for the man who sent those flowers, which was the largest display, but nobody in the family had ever heard of him. So, if the florist wanted to plod ahead, they would have to do an extensive investigation on Albert Hornstein to ferret out any connection to the man in his life. The florist thought about it, and decided to drop it at this point. Mac's curiosity certainly was aroused, but this was the end of the line.

Fortunately, it was not the end of the line for other matters. That afternoon the telephone ringing drew Mac away from the computer. She knew immediately from the deep voice that it was Andrew. "I am interested in hiring a female detective to help me determine whether the food served at dinner at a particular restaurant is as good as it is advertised to be. Might she be available?"

"Possibly. Do you have character references?"

"I am a character, you can be assured of that."

"How about your credit?"

"I don't get enough of that."

"Let me check her schedule. When is this investigation planned for?"

"Saturday night, at 7:30."

"Hold on." Mac turned to Tom with a broad smile as he gave a thumb's up. "Looks good."

"Wonderful. Where can I pick her up?"

"Professionally, before you sign client commitment papers, she has to meet you at the place."

"So be it. It is The Lonesome Duck, 515 La Grosse."

"And, your name?"

"Iaman Undertaker. And her name?"

"Itremains Tobeseen."

FIFTEEN

Before leaving for the restaurant, Mac looked at herself in the full length mirror in her room. With her long black hair and wide black eyes, a simple black dress was a good choice. She guessed black would be an undertaker's favorite color. The only jewelry she ever wore was a watch, and she did not use makeup or even lipstick. It was premised on her belief that for her to be as natural as possible she should look that way as well. She also refused to wear high heel shoes, finding them unnecessarily uncomfortable. Women punished themselves in fashion and her nonconformism freed her from such painful restrictions. A small heel height was her limit, and it had worked for her until now so there was no reason to change anything. She would be as short as she was just as Andrew would be as tall as he was. A lesson learned from Tommy was that people had to accept her on her terms, as she was. If they had trouble doing that, such was their problem.

Mac tried to be punctual for commitments. Being fashionably late was too pretentious, another poise that made no sense. So, at 7:30 she opened the door to the restaurant, and Andrew was waiting for her there. He was dressed casually, and he greeted her with a broad smile. "Hello, you sweet and adorable woman."

She smiled. "How do you know me so well?"

He smiled back. "An educated guess from what I have determined so far. I waited for you here before getting a table."

"Kind of you."

After being seated, he remarked, "You sure are one pretty detective."

"Pretty good, too."

"I am sure."

"I think you have been around dead bodies for so long that a live one has taken you by surprise."

"A pleasant one, at that."

"Have you ever had a dead body come back to life?"

"You watch too many movies."

"I don't watch many movies. Just an active imagination."

"Can you imagine we not talk about what we do but who we are."

A knowing smile. "One in the same in the end, but I get your drift."

The dinner was good, and Mac enjoyed the food and the pleasant conversation. She talked more about Tommy than about herself, realizing she really had not done much to brag about in her twenty-seven years until the prospect of change presented itself with the guru. She found herself describing her life in two phases – BT (before Tommy) and AT (after Tommy). Andrew, on the other hand, talked much about himself, and Mac had the impression that being an undertaker was another form of a lonely life with little opportunity to talk about himself. He had a sheltered childhood, and his future was preordained to be a part of the family business. His sister, Gloria, more rebellious than Andrew attempted at an early stage to exert an independence but that was quickly and completely squelched. Being only fifteen months apart in age, they did much together and had always been best friends. Gloria also had little chance for outside socialization and was unmarried. The two lived at home with their retired father and overbearing mother. Andrew was candid in stating that at an earlier period before he was immersed in the funeral business he was interested in becoming a chef. That dream had to be abandoned along with any other expectations not pertaining to the family business. Having a gourmet dinner such as this one brought about a sense of missing out on true accomplishment and satisfaction. He did not state it outright, but it was obvious that the compulsion of family history was overbearing.

"Mac stared into those hazel eyes. "You need to meet and listen to Tommy, my boss. He is guiding me to dream big time, as well as to live a life all my own."

"Sounds like a strong person."

"He is my guru, my man on the mountain top. He is eighty-two but as old as time and as young as hope." It gave her a thrill just to talk about Tommy, and she was sure he could lead Andrew as well out of his shell.

He looked into those piercing black eyes believing that he had finally met a person he could open up to, a person he could listen to. "You are right."

"It is not a case of being right. One does not have to be a detective to know that you need to do something before it is too late."

He was going to say it was already too late, but he did not want her to see that he was emotionally weak. "I think much of your boss has rubbed off on you."

"I hope so."

After dinner they took a walk. The conversation continued with long periods of relaxed silence. When they returned to her car, she thanked him and kissed him on the cheek. In as sultry a voice as she could muster, she said, "Call me again, if you wish."

He smiled. "That will be on the top of any wish list I might make."

Andrew watched as she drove away, and his mind was suddenly

full of wishes. Just perhaps there was some room in his life for a little something else.

SIXTEEN

On Monday Mac filled Tommy in on the date with Andrew. By that time, she had thought it all through. Andrew was nice, but there was no intense feeling towards him and, upon reflection, some of the conversation they had was forced. Tom's reaction was as she might have guessed. "Love rarely comes all at once. More often than not, it grows slowly but surely. Give the poor guy a chance. He spends most of his time in a controlled and restricted environment, and it takes a sexy secretary to unlock any hidden treasures."

"Reasonable, I suppose. Yet, he is no Tommy."

"There is only one Tommy and one Mac. There is, rather there should be, always room in your heart for others."

"That goes for you as well."

"Yes, it does."

Tom had not telephoned April for a week. He was tempted to do so a few times although he really was hoping she would reach out to him. As far as he knew, she had not yet told any of the children about their new living arrangement. He figured she was waiting for a development to either solidify the move or his plea to come back. He was at peace, so she was calling the shots.

The trip with Adele was next week. He made a list of the things he should do now.

Ship the gun to the hotel.

Take best suit to the dry cleaners.
Call Adele to check with her if there
was anything else he should do or bring.
Make sure apartment is clean for Mac.

That night he dreamed again that had implications and was suggestive of him dying. This time he was at the insurance company and he was working with his team on a major project. As if he knew he was going to die before the project was completed, he reviewed which member of the team was best to lead it on. The image of Mac emerged, again with a double rainbow beyond her shoulder. The significance was obvious. His reliance on the young woman was growing daily, and it dawned on him that he was grooming her to carry on with his life's efforts when he would no longer be able to do so. He made a mental note to tell Mac about the concept of reliance. The reliance her mother had on her was only one kind of reliance. A certain reliance imbued with trust can be a form of love. It was the recognition that the person is an alter ego.

When he awoke from the dream, he pondered more about his own death. It was more than just leaving things uncompleted, it was the finality of it. He was not a believer in an after life, and it would just be an ending over which he had no control and no knowledge. Yet, he could and should prepare for its consequences. He would need to prepare a detailed listing of the joint assets for April. Depending where their relationship was now going, he would have to revise their wills. He had two substantial life insurance policies. One would be sufficient for April considering the other death benefits and the stocks and bonds. He would make Mac the beneficiary of the other one. That way she would have the funds to carry on the business or to have the independence to follow her own dreams. Freedom of choice is a valuable legacy.

Tom knew his dreaming had not ended, and there would undoubtedly be future dreams about death which would lead him to additional thoughts. Old folks have a tendency to dwell on concepts, new ones as well as those lurking in the shadows. Young people think about most things only long enough to decide what they want to do. What they need to do or should do is on the second level of decision-making. He needed to show Mac that the second level of thinking should be the first-level.

SEVENTEEN

"Perhaps, he is not interested in me at all," Mac announced to Tommy a few days later. "He hasn't called."

"Ah, lass, impatience can be a sign of desire. Maybe, he made more of an impression on you than you care to admit."

"No, that's not it. I just believed him when he said he would call."

"Ah, lass, then call him before you pop a blood vessel."

"I don't want him to think I am that interested."

"Then, just wait it out. If he never calls your problem is solved. You need not deal with him or confront your own feelings."

"I see what you are doing."

"I knew you would."

"Limbo is for a dumbo."

"I couldn't have put it any better."

She thought for a moment. "I think I'll just go over there and pretend I have another question to ask him about the flowers."

"A plan, although not iron-clad. What if he asks you why you just would not have called?"

"I'll tell him I was driving by when the question came to me."

"Fishy, but reel him in, junior sleuth."

As luck would have it, when Mac drove over to the funeral home there were no cars in the parking lot so Andrew would not be tied up with a funeral. Again, there was nobody around when she entered the vestibule. She shouted out, "Andrew, are you here?"

Shortly, a young woman came out from the back. "Hello, I am Andrew's sister, may I help you?"

"Oh, hello. I am Mac Greenmore from the Thomas Lloyd Detective Agency. I spoke with Andrew last week about a mysterious flower arrangement for one of your funerals."

"Yes, he told me about it. Are you the woman he went to dinner with on Saturday?"

"I am. Nice to meet you."

"I am Gloria. Come back to my office so we can chat."

Mac followed her through the door to what was probably a meeting and conference room with a series of offices off of it. All the office doors were closed except one which turned out to be Gloria's. Once inside, Gloria sat by a table and motioned for Mac to sit in one of the other chairs. "Can I get you a cup of coffee or a bottle of water?"

"No, thanks. Is Andrew not in today?"

"This may sound strange, and don't get me wrong, I love my brother dearly, but he is a very unusual person."

"What do you mean?"

"I am sure you have made some of your own judgments about him already. He has some idiosyncrasies."

"Don't we all?"

Gloria was as tall as Andrew and strikingly beautiful. Short brown hair framed a perfectly unblemished oval face. "In varying degrees, I am sure. My brother tests the limits. One unfathomable trait is a knack for disappearing for days at a time. Nobody knows where he has gone or what he may be doing. He'll show up again with no explanations, no answers to questions. He was here Monday morning, told me about his dinner with you, and I have not seen or heard from him since."

"Maybe, it is a basic discontentment with the business."

"That is probably part of it. I know he would rather be doing something else. So would I except the whole family is dependent on us to run the business, and it is very lucrative."

"The one thing I keep learning is that money is not everything."

"Perhaps, not. However, it goes a long way when you get used to creature comforts."

"Leaving money aside, what would you like to do?"

Gloria was quiet for a moment. Mac assumed it had been a thought-provoking question. "Funny you should ask that." A moment's pause. "When I was in college, which seems a long time ago, and I suppose it was in more than one way since it has been more than ten years, I was intrigued by criminal justice. I even took a course in forensics and related subjects."

"What did you major in?"

"Psychology. What did you major in?"

"I only went to college for a year. I can't sit still."

"My mind does not sit still?"

"Have you ever thought about becoming a detective?"

"Some detective I would make. I can't even find out why or where Andrew disappears to. What made you want to be a detective?"

"It appeals to me. Then I met Tommy, my boss, and he is my mentor. Through him I don't stop learning. Not just about the world of investigations. He has opened my eyes to life. He is elderly and wise. You should meet him."

"I would like that. First, when Andrew shows up I'll tell him to call you as he should get to know you better. You would be good for him. For me, too. Maybe, we can be friends."

"A good idea. The way I see it, you both are far too involved in death."

Gloria stood up and came over to Mac and hugged her. "You

are right about that."

EIGHTEEN

It was Monday morning when Mac answered the telephone. "Thomas Lloyd Detective Agency."

"Mac, is that you?"

"Yes."

"This is Gloria Nathan. Andrew still has not returned. I am getting worried. He has never been gone this long. Can you help me to find him?"

"Hold on." Mac turned to Tommy and told him what Gloria said.

"Get the home address and ask her if she could meet us there so we can check out Andrew's living space. First, ask her to check his office for anything that might help, especially what might be on his computer."

Gloria could not find anything helpful in Andrew's office. They both used the same password for their computers, but they were used strictly for the business. She set out to the house to wait for Tom and Mac.

The Nathan residence was in the elite part of the city. A large manicured lawn, a circular driveway, and a huge three-story house surrounded by palm trees. "I would disappear from here, too," Tom uttered as they went up the driveway.

Gloria was waiting in the front of the house. She led them in to the massive interior of the imposing home, ornate decorations everywhere. She escorted them up the wide staircase to the third level where Andrew had his bedroom and a large sitting room which was filled with antiques. Floor to ceiling shelves housed objects small and large apparently grouped by their early usage. Tom could barely catch his breath from the stair climbing. "I don't miss stairs, that's for sure."

The father came up to meet them. "So, you are the folks going to locate my wayward son?"

Mac answered quickly, "If we can."

The father responded, "I am James Nathan. I don't understand my son, and I equally think he does not understand me. Instead of thanking me for a good life, he fights me every inch of the way."

"I am Tom, and this is Mac. Perhaps, there is more than one definition of a good life."

The elder Nathan's response was gruff. "I don't understand that either. Young folks should stay on the road well traveled."

It was Mac who emphatically spoke up. "There are times we need to make a new road."

"What for?"

"For change; for challenges."

"I'll never understand that either. Anyway, do what you can and give me your bill." With that he turned and started down the stairs.

Gloria spoke just as soon as her father was out of sight. "He is not as hard as he seems. As he admits, he just does not understand."

Tom offered, "The old school is surrounded by deep and at times impenetrable trenches. A different kind of impatience settles in a senior's heart, but an impatience after all. I see there is a computer. Do you know Andrew's password for this one?"

"No."

"Any guesses?"

"Not really."

Mac suggested, "Let me try your business one as well as some obvious ones just in the case of a case." None worked.

They looked through Andrew's desk and belongings. Nothing peaked their interest, so they left promising Gloria they would delve into it. Tom's parting advice was for Gloria to file a missing person's report with the police.

In the car on the way back to the office, Tom asked Mac candidly, "Are you earnest about finding Andrew?"

Her answer was quick, perhaps a bit too quick. "Yes, for Gloria."

"Between now and Thursday when you need to drive me and Adele to the airport and get yourself settled in the apartment, the one obvious clue as to his whereabouts is the antiques. He probably spends the time, or at least part of the time, hunting for those obsessive objects. Compile a list of antiques malls and shops in the State and adjoining Georgia, and start calling them asking if they know of him and if so have they seen him recently. Start with the malls. The selections are more numerous and he might have a tendency to linger there longer. If any pan out, contact motels nearby to find out if he is or was registered there."

"Why didn't I think of that?"

"That is why there are two of us. Only one of us has to have an idea at a time."

"I hope you don't ever charge me for learning from you. It would push indebtedness to the max."

"Nonsense. All you would have to do is to dig in the pot of gold at the end of one of the double rainbows to compensate me."

"When we get back to the office I'm going to give you the biggest hug you ever had as a down payment."

"Then, I am already a rich man."

NINETEEN

"I never would have guessed there were so many antique places," Mac blurted out the next day. "Antiques must be more popular than I ever imagined."

"Not as popular as plentiful, although the quest to find something of great value at a bargain price probably has appeal. Old items were built or made to last, and last they do. People are just the reverse, not built to last and when their use ends so does their value."

"I know nothing about antiques."

"You can't be an expert about everything, and a smattering of knowledge can often be dangerous. However, learn all you can when you can. You just never know when that can become useful."

"Anyway, it will take forever to contact them all."

"You may get lucky. Just keep track of it all as the elder Nathan said he will pay our bill. And, fit in the other case work as well."

"Phew! This is supposed to be fun, not work."

"Disappointed?"

"No. Just reality is a slap in the face."

"Good for the complexion."

Wednesday night as Tom was packing for the wedding trip his mind wandered. He thought about April, and he was not sure he was more sorry for her or for himself. You cannot be together for so many years and shared so many life experiences without some close and intimate feeling taking hold. Even if in the final analysis it is not love, it may be as close to that as many people might get. Very few other women would probably have put up with him for as long as she had. He would be the first one to admit that. He had no doubt she had been faithful to him as he had been with her. There had been great satisfaction in the parenting department and raising good and now productive children is no easy task. So, he had returned to the mental debate on the subject of wasting one's life. Can it be deemed a waste if there was value, perhaps even great value, in the sense of a feeling of satisfaction in a substantive accomplishment being with a person for a major portion of a lifetime although it was not an abiding love? Love is probably not the only criteria of a worthy life, although it is and should be a major aspect. Tom knew he would go round and round with this concerning his own life. A greater dilemma is what would he say to Mac if she asked him about it.

With such intense mental scrutiny, little wonder his convoluted dreams that night led him to situations where decisions involved romantic considerations. Predicting consequences was confusing and frustrating, and the only conclusion he could draw from it was that he, as a matter of fact, knew even less about it than he originally thought. He could hardly guide himself and it would be dangerously insensitive to attempt to give Mac any advice. He would not want to tarnish the image of wisdom that she had of him, but as a distinct matter of practicality as well as theory he was far from that posture. One of the feats he needed to complete before he departed this world would be to try and live up to her opinion of him. That meant gaining some smarts each day so that in effect he would be wiser than the day before but not as wise as tomorrow. An intriguing part of the journey to tomorrow. Certainly a worthwhile goal although it might be biting off more than he could chew. Would he live long enough to find out for sure?

TWENTY

Driving over to pick up Adele, Mac remarked, "Sure am going to miss you, Tommy."

"Ditto, lass, but you will be so busy you will hardly notice I am gone. It is a short flight to Charleston, and you will pick us up on Sunday."

"I don't know about that. The inspiration will be lacking, and no entries in the wisdom journal."

"Be inspired to find Andrew."

"Barely making a dent in that department."

"I have an idea. Let's recruit Gloria to become a private investigator. Give her a part of the list and let her make those calls. Also, ask her to comb through Andrew's desk to look for any purchase receipt for an antique that might have the shop information on it. That might shorten the hunt."

"You are chock full of good ideas. By the way, thanks again for letting me stay at the apartment, even though it will add to the emptiness of your absence."

"Absence makes the heart grow fonder."

"I'm fondered out."

Adele was waiting by the front door of the nursing home, suitcase by her side. The flowered dress hung loosely on the overly skinny frame, and spindly legs looked unlikely to hold the body frame for any length of time. The thin gray hair was neatly in place. Tom thought to himself, "I will be spending most of the time holding her up in more ways than one."

They did not talk much during the brief flight. Tom could tell she was feeling a bunch of mixed emotions, and as long as she did not initiate a conversation he thought it best to let her address it all on her own, at least for now.

As Ellie had promised, a limousine was waiting at the Charleston Airport to take them to the hotel. The same limousine would be taking them to the plantation on Saturday for the wedding and then back to the hotel afterward, as well as taking them to the Airport on Sunday.

Tom did not know how many surprises there might be this weekend, but the first one was a big one. At the hotel, Adele had changed the reservation from two adjoining rooms to one room with twin beds as he had jokingly remarked would save her money. "As long as I am paying for a body guard, I might as well make it full time," her voice trailed off but there was a hint of a smile on her face.

Actually, Tom was delighted with the idea. Not only did he want to assure she was protected, he had a desire to be with her and to concentrate on building up her self worth. It also showed once again that she had spunk. Old age risk taking can have great rewards.

At the front desk, they picked up the package that he had shipped containing the gun as well as the special dress Ellie had gotten for Adele for the wedding. They had a light lunch at the hotel after settling in the room. The hotel was located in the downtown section of Charleston, a city filled with quaint shops and fine restaurants. After taking a guided bus tour of the City to absorb all of the rich history of the place, they walked around the area near the hotel. Adele had more energy than he had given her credit for. They came upon an interesting looking Italian restaurant and made a reservation there for dinner that night so they might compare the eggplant parmigiano with the one they had back home.

Back in the room, Adele telephoned Ellie and they had a long animated conversation. Ellie and Candice would be meeting them for breakfast at the hotel. They wanted to check and make sure everything was set for the rehearsal dinner there that night as well.

After a nap, they watched the news on television and dressed for dinner. The atmosphere was relaxed, and if one did not know the actual situation one would have guessed that the two were a long time married couple.

At dinner, where the food was enjoyable and the atmosphere soothing and unrushed, they had their first serious conversation. Tom initiated the discussion. "Dear heart, do you believe in an afterlife?"

Her response was emphatic. "No, I do not."

"Then, why are you looking forward to dying?"

"It is the best solution all around."

"For your ex maybe, not for you."

"For me, especially." She took off her glasses. "Look in my eyes. What do you see?"

"Ha, that's an easy one. I see a vibrant woman who is alive to her depths, with a daughter and grandchildren beckoning her to join them. I see a woman who wants and needs to do much more before the final curtain."

She reached out her hand to cover his hand that was leaning on the table. The skin was cold and crusty. "Your fee does not cover lying. I will tell you what is really there. I am a frail and sickly woman who takes more than a dozen pills every day just to keep up the basic functions. Other than my daughter and the grandchildren, I have experienced a lifetime of smashed emotions and fragmented feelings, many moments of frustration and disappointment, and an overwhelming disgust with myself for letting it happen and not being able to do anything about it. I gave up the will to fight back early and could never regain control of my life. I never knew who I was, and never found a way to determine who I could be or even who I was meant to be. That is why death is the answer. It will end my suffering and torment."

When he was sure she was finished, he spoke softly. "I don't see it or you that way. You still have time and the ability to seek and feel happiness. It is never too late to find the missing pieces and to fit them together to form the picture of a brighter tomorrow. It may not make up for all of the unhappy years and the misery, but it can go a long way to make things better. There are many positives for you to concentrate on. Ellie and her children want you to be there to share in their lives and accomplishments. You should want that as well. You still have your mental faculties, you are bright and witty, and utterly charming I might add. There is much that is appealing about you."

She interrupted him. "Don't you find me ugly, even grotesque?"

"Not by a long shot. Maybe some fat could be added to the bones," he noted a faint trace of a smile on her face, "But to me you are a magnificent woman."

"You are certainly crazy as a loon. You keep demonstrating that to me. Maybe, early in life, I should have sought out crazy men."

It was his turn to smile. "We can be crazy together."

She tightened her grip on his hand, and he covered her hand with his other hand. She drained the wine from the glass. Perhaps, it was the alcohol, perhaps it was something else. All of a sudden, crazy sounded awfully good to her.

TWENTY-ONE

It was a cool evening. Tom and Adele walked back to the hotel at a leisurely pace, noting the festive mood of the people they passed. They stopped numerous times looking in the windows of the shops and discussing the items on display. Adele had read much to fill in on a lonely past, and a built-up repertory of knowledge was evident once it was tapped. A fertile mind does not necessarily lose its capacity because it has aged. In fact, it might be just the opposite. It can foster new growth and additional bountiful harvests.

"I have never talked so much before."

"You should do it more often. It is a pleasure listening to you."

"You are crazy, no doubt about it. I am surprised you have not been locked up and the key thrown away."

"Telling it like it is a special kind of craziness, undetectable except by receptive hearts and minds."

In the room, Tom spoke with a flare, "It has been a full and enjoyable day, dear heart. Now, I will take a shower, which I do at night instead of in the morning. I hope it does not shock you, but I sleep in the nude. A habit perpetuated in my youth and reinforced by the heat and humidity of Hilton Head. It liberates my spirit and tantalizes my dreams."

She laughed. "Nothing you say or do shocks me. A crazy old man can and should do what he likes. I promise I won't look. If I don't have my glasses on even if I look I can't see anything clearly. I also take a shower at night. It helps to wash away the troubles of the day."

"You have already seen the best parts of me."

"You have already seen all of the parts of me."

It had been a long day, and as the shower water cascaded over his old hulk it felt good. The hotel had large fluffy towels, and for a moment he lingered in the lap of luxury. He would not want to get used to it. Such was not his style or within the reasonable realm of his expectations. However, he could ably handle a moment here and there.

Tom lay in the bed and closed his eyes. He heard the shower, and sleep came easily. A sound, a sigh as best he could describe it, awakened him. The room was dark. He sensed the sheet being lifted as a naked Adele got in the bed with him. He moved over so she would have adequate room. "Please, just hold me," was her whispered wish.

He enfolded his arms around her, fully aware of rough, sagging skin that was cold to the touch. He clutched her body to him, warming the flesh. She was so thin he could have held two of her. It had been a sigh he had heard because he heard another one. He smelled the soap in her hair as he had when they had gone to lunch back home, and he caressed a body barely there. A very special contentment transitioned to a gentle and deep sleep.

When he awoke, it was light outside although the heavy drapes on the window cast the room in dark shadows. She was still in his arms staring at him. "Good morning," she said in a hushed whisper as if she did not want anyone else to hear.

"Good morning."

"I had a wonderful sleep. I dreamed that a kind man was loving me."

"Dreams are far better than reality."

"I told him how much I appreciated him and how much I loved him.   He told me he loved me, too."

"He does love you."

"Please, don't ever wake me up."

TWENTY-TWO

Adele reached for Tom's hand as they rode down in the elevator to meet Ellie and Candice for breakfast. "I didn't tell Ellie I hired you or that you are a private detective. I just told her we have been seeing each other socially."

Fingers intertwined comfortably. "Works for me."

Ellie and Candice were already at a table in the hotel's restaurant. After hugs and introductions, breakfast was ordered. Ellie was a petite woman, sort of like Mac, and Tom could sense immediately the affection she had for Adele. Candice took after her mother, and had a warm and endearing smile. "Grandma, you should have told us earlier that you had a fella. We could have made this a double wedding."

"Sure are no family secrets around here," Adele chirped in jovially. "Besides, at our age, there are no weddings. We just share medicines."

"Well, Tom," Ellie beamed, "You can tell that this family revolves around your wedding companion."

"I see that clearly," Tom offered. "Looks like I am getting more than I bargained for."

The breakfast and conversation were pleasant. Candice talked mainly about the wedding and her intended, and Ellie described her pupils and related stories about the rest of the family, all of whom would be at the wedding. Ellie's father would not be at the rehearsal dinner. Adele was spared from any confrontation until the next day.

Ellie and Candice went on to check on the preparations for the rehearsal dinner. Tom and Adele went back to the room, which had already been made up.

"I am going to call Mac while you decide what you would like to do today."

"Tommy, I was hoping you would call. I love it at the apartment. I feel you are everywhere. Even at the office you are there. You sure get around. I am too busy to be jealous that you are with another woman. Still no luck finding Andrew. Gloria is thrilled to help, although she did not find any receipts for any antiques. She has two funerals today, and two tomorrow, so Andrew is on hold."

Tom felt he needed to calm her down. "Let it all slide to Monday and I'll pitch in. Take the weekend off, relax and unwind. You can add apartment sitter to your resume."

Adele was standing at the window staring out at the harbor. Tom came up behind her and kissed the back of her neck as he held on to her firmly. "Well, you adorable old lady, have you decided what you would like to do today? The rehearsal is not until 5:00."

She turned to face him. "I would like you to kiss me and take me to bed."

He bent down and gently kissed the thin lips. She leaned in to him, pressing the thin frame to him as he kissed her again with greater ardor. He closed the drapes and in the dim light undressed her. Her trembling hands undressed him. They got in the bed and held on to each other. The silence was pervasive. The significance was overpowering.

They dozed in this relaxed mode for a couple of hours, dressed, and went out for a walk. Still full from breakfast they decided to skip lunch, although they did get an ice cream cone from one of the shops.

When they returned to the room they dressed for the dinner

that proved to be pleasant and enjoyable. Candice's intended was polite and obviously quite smitten with her. His family was friendly and warm, and their wealth did not seem to be any barrier for the expected union.

"Are you anxious about tomorrow?", Tom asked after they showered together and got in the bed.

"Not with you at my side." Adele responded stroking his cheek. "I have never felt this sure of myself. That will guarantee this as a happy time. I actually think I am experiencing what true happiness is and can be."

"That is what the doctor ordered."

"You will be glad to hear this. It makes me want to live."

"That is what I ordered."

"I love you, my private detective."

"I love you as well, my private treasure."

"Do you love me enough to waive all the fees?"

"Don't push it, lady."

They both laughed. A memorable kiss led to a long embrace in a peaceful night.

TWENTY-THREE

The idea hatched when Mac discovered that the sofa in the living room was a convertible sofa. If her mother would be able to shift for herself, Mac would ask Tommy if she could live in the apartment with him. Two for the ages would be two for the here and now.

Thoughts about Andrew were disjointed. The mystery of his disappearance shrouded any personal feelings she might have towards him. If nothing else, the last thing she would need or want would be for a romantic involvement with a man who had a tendency to disappear for periods of time. As close as she could figure it, some mental weakness would be the trigger for such behavior. She did not mind being a daughter to Tommy, but she would not want to be a mother to Andrew.

Mac called Gloria and invited her over to the apartment after the funerals and they would order in a pizza. Gloria was more than happy to accept. As attractive as she was, she had practically no social life. As with Andrew, the only unmarried men she met were through the funerals and dating was not on their minds.

After Gloria arrived, Mac called in to order the pizza delivery. While they waited, they talked about a host of subjects. There was still no news about Andrew, and Gloria promised to start making calls on Monday. After a lull in the conversation, Gloria inquired, "Tell me about your childhood."

"Not much to tell, and even less to boast about. I was a loner in school. I had few friends because I shied away from typical girl interests. My father ran away with another woman, so the home life was shattered. I have been trying to pick up the pieces ever since. How about you?"

"Also, not much to relate. Not much worth remembering. The funeral business always seemed to spill over to the home, and if there was a good week there then things were calm at the house. If it was a bad financial week, there was much tension in the surroundings and Andrew and I were often ignored. We were not allowed to have friends over, so few stuck with us. Have you had any serious heartthrobs?"

"Not worth reciting. Until now when my biological clock is winding down, I considered men more of a nuisance than anything else. Tommy has shown me differently, and has led me to believe there can be so much more than a physical relationship."

"I learned that the hard way."

"How so?"

"I had two boy friends when I was in college. Both were handsome, popular, but emotionally and intellectually shallow. Sex was their primary interest, and there was constant pressure. I never enjoyed it, was never satisfied. It has left me disappointed and discouraged."

"Ah, what might have been. Tommy would say, not necessarily what might be."

Gloria spoke jovially, "I'll make a deal with you. Whichever one of us finds a promising prospect, make sure he has an eligible friend."

"That will work. The ideal for me would be to find a younger version of Tommy."

"You might have to settle for less."

"Settle is not an option. I rather do without than to not have it all."

"I believe all options should be on the table."

"Not my table."

TWENTY-FOUR

They dressed for the wedding after having a light breakfast at the hotel. Tom detected a slight trembling of Adele's body as he hugged her. "Apprehensive?"

"A little, I suppose. I would like to get it behind me so I can enjoy the day and being with you."

"If it is any comfort, I will not leave your side."

"It is the greatest comfort."

"You look beautiful in that dress."

"Flattery will not get you a tip."

"Shucks! You do look wonderful."

"I am happy, a new sensation for me. So, even if not true, I can feel beautiful."

"That, dear lady, is the secret to an acceptable life. Let your mind and heart control who you are meant to be."

The limousine was waiting in the street by the hotel. It was a forty-five minute trip to the plantation. The day was warm and clear and held much promise for a successful wedding event. The picturesque venue added just the right touch for the festivities.

Mel Scheinfeld was already there when they arrived. Adele let out a gasp, not one of apprehension but of utter surprise. Instead of the robust and healthy man she had known in the marriage years, he was now something of a pathetic figure and not one to be fearful of. He had gained substantial weight and his movements were awkward and certainly not menacing. Perhaps, his impression of her was the same. He looked away as they approached the area he was in, and it was evident that he was going to ignore her rather than confront her. That was fine as far as she was concerned. All of the years that she had considered him an overpowering figure, and now she sensed she had worried about nothing. She did not really need Tom as a protector, just as an object of her affection.

Adele could not have wished for a better day. Once the perceived threat was removed from the event, she was absorbed in the joy and significance of the day. The ongoing attention and involvement of Ellie and the grandchildren spread warmth in her heart, and the feel of Tom's presence filled her with confidence and the desire to be a full participant in all that surrounded her. Because of all of the positives, the wonderful day for Adele made it that way for Tom as well.

At the end of the evening Ellie came up to him and hugged him. "Thank you from the bottom of my heart for making my mother so happy."

"Little lady, if you only knew. Your mother has done even more for me."

It was late by the time they arrived back at the hotel. They showered and fell into an exhausted sleep. Before she closed her eyes, Adele caressed Tom's cheek. "For so many reasons, this has been the happiest day of my life. Most of all, dearest, I discovered I can fit a tall man in my heart. Funny, for so long I thought I had no heart at all. Now, I have discovered it is the most vital part of me. Will you stay in there?"

"Gladly" as he gently kissed her aging fingers.

On the plane, he held her hand. "By the way, I am waiving my fee. You have already made me a rich man. You will, although, have to pay twenty-five percent which is Mac's share."

Her voice was low and raspy. "Thank you. You are kind to an old lady. You let me know that amount for Mac and I will have Florence send you a check on my behalf. I don't have a need for an account for myself."

Mac was dutifully waiting for them at the airport. Her eyebrows raised slightly as she saw them holding hands as they came through the gate. She smiled as Adele was so talkative all the way back to the nursing home. Tom carried Adele's suitcase to the door and they kissed.

"Well. Tommy," Mac remarked as he got back in the car, "I hope I find Andrew as easily as you rescued a lost soul."

"It may have started out that way, but I have found love with this woman."

"Are you sure you don't just feel sorry for her."

"I am sure. In all of my years, I have never had this kind of passion for a person, words really are inadequate to express it. A new discovery at any age is exciting. For an old person it borders on hysteria. It boggles my mind when I realize what I have been missing all of these years. Now, you must find this kind of love so you can bask in it for a lifetime."

"Easier said then done."

"Perhaps, but knowing it can exist will make the hunt that more exciting."

TWENTY-FIVE

Tom let Mac stay over and agreed to have her live there if it all worked out with her mother. He knew she would do her part, and he was getting used to having her around for dinner and as meaningful and entertaining company. It would be easier to guide her if there was more peaceful time to devote to the endeavor. Privacy for an old man is no big deal, and he would respect her privacy as well. Sharing the one bathroom might be a problem, but it did not have to be.

Monday morning brought a surprise. Gloria called Mac to tell her that Andrew had reappeared. He acted as if he had not been gone and would not talk about his absence. Mac would prepare the final bill and take it over to the father. She would ask Andrew for some answers. She felt she deserved that much.

At the house, James Nathan wrote out a check. Andrew and Gloria had already left for the funeral home. Mac drove there and went directly to Andrew's office. He seemed surprised to see her. "Mac, what are you doing here?"

"You may not have explained yourself to your family, but I would like to know why you disappeared and where to."

He was calm and pointed to a chair. "Sit and I will tell you."

Gloria heard the commotion and came in. "I want to hear this, too."

"I was planning to make an announcement at dinner tonight so you would have heard it all then. You sit as well and you can have a preview."

Mac was stern. "You better make it good."

"Good is relative. It's good for me. First, you are the one who motivated me to leave."

"Me?", Mac interrupted a bit perturbed.

"Yes, you. You got me to thinking about what I should be doing with my life. So, I needed to go somewhere quiet so I could think things through. Asheville, North Carolina is my favorite place. Besides the Biltmore House my favorite antiques mall is there. There is also a culinary school in the city. So, I lost myself there, mulled things over and have decided I want to be a chef. I enrolled in the school. The session starts in September."

"Good for you," Mac offered.

"Not so good for me," Gloria interjected.

"Nonsense," Andrew retorted. "You are capable of running the business by yourself, and pops would lend a hand if things get too burdensome."

"And what if I want to go off and do something else?"

"Which I would encourage if that is a path you desire. I know the business means much to the family, but maybe, just maybe after all, it is time to sell it off and everyone can be free to do whatever they want."

Gloria scowled. "You leave me in an awkward position. They will forgive you if you take off. Once you have, they will not understand if I want to bow out as well."

"Sorry. I should have done this long ago, and I need to do it now."

"Dinner is going to prove to be very interesting. Mac, would you like to come to dinner and see the fireworks?"

"You can tell me all about it afterwards. I don't want to get involved. I would be for sure labeled the bad guy."

"To the contrary," Andrew chimed in. "You have merely opened my eyes. A savior of sorts."

"I'll watch the video."

TWENTY-SIX

Upon returning from the wedding, Adele had debated with herself about her decision. It became a final one after Tom's Sunday visit to the nursing home. She had given him the check Florence had written to cover the expenses for Mac. She and Tom walked the grounds of the home and sat on a bench under a tree. They held hands, and he would stroke the back of her hand with tenderness. They were mainly quiet, and it was a calming peace.

The pain was getting worse, so much so that the medications were of little help. As part of her decision she had stopped taking all of her medications a few days ago anyway. In what seemed like a flash of time she had experienced a surge of happiness at Candice's wedding and a great love with Tom. Now, to spare them all from seeing her suffering and not being able to do anything about it, she needed to depart from this world while those two events bolstered her resolve. She would not be a burden to anyone. She had to write two letters – one to Ellie and one to Tom.

My Dear Ellie:

When you read this I will no longer be here. What I am doing may appear selfish, but I am doing it out of my love for you and your family. My pain is increasing and cannot be controlled. My physical and mental capabilities are diminishing. I know you would lovingly take care of me if you could, although that would just be prolonging my suffering and agony. I do not want to be a burden. I want you to devote your entire energy and concern on your wonderful family.

I take with me the memory of a wonderful and loving daughter, the one bright spot in an otherwise dark and unforgiving life. If you keep me in your heart I will be with you always.

With an eternal embrace,

Mom

Tom, my dear, dear Tom:

When you read this I will be gone. Forgive me for my body leaving you. My pain and suffering lead me to do for you what I cannot do for myself. The tears flowed when you offered to have me stay with you so you could take care of me. It is even a monumental job for the nursing home staff. My love for you cannot and should not be a burden.

I thought I would die without experiencing a great love. I do die having had that love, and I take it with me. I have loved you like I always thought I could love. Better yet, I had the grand feeling of being loved. It would have been wonderful to have had it for a long time, but its significance to me was not diminished by the brevity of time. Sweet and gentle man, I take your love with me in death. That way I will always have a form of life – for love is life. I leave with you the only possession I truly have – my love for you. It will look out over you. It is my legacy.

Holding you and being held by you forever,

Adele

When Mac answered the telephone, the woman at the other end of the line was sobbing, "Let me talk to Tom, please."

"This is Tom."

"Tom, this is Ellie. The home just called. Mom has died."

Tom dropped the receiver. Old men cry as much as anyone else, maybe even more. Mac knew immediately what had happened and came to cradle him. She cried with him, sensing his loss.

TWENTY-SEVEN

There was a third letter. Florence opened it when she found Adele who had died in her sleep. It thanked her for all she had done, especially the close cousin care, and upon her death to call Ellie. Florence locked the door to Adele's room until Ellie could get there to say goodbye to her mother. When Tom arrived first, she let him in the room and gave him the envelope addressed to him.

Adele looked peaceful. He also thought she looked beautiful. He kissed the cold lips, sat by the window and read the letter. He wept for the three hours that it took Ellie to drive from Charleston. They hugged and cried together.

Ellie opened her letter and the sobs increased. Florence had already arranged for the crematorium to retrieve the body as Ellie had arranged early on when the event ever took place. After the body was removed, Tom and Ellie hugged before she started on her drive back to Charleston. They agreed that Tom would hold on to the ashes until it was decided what to do with them.

Back at the office, Mac hugged Tommy firmly. She felt his pain, and that too was revealing. Joined souls have common feelings, mutual empathy.

Tom did not tell any of this to April when they talked. In a way, it defied description. It would have been unnecessarily mean to tell her anyway. Her notion that they had a long and successful marriage until the recent division should be something for her to hold on to even if he was now convinced otherwise. The thought expressed by Adele that even a brief monumental love is a crowning achievement echoed in his soul.

"I have no romantic interest in Andrew," Mac stated as they sat down for dinner that night in the apartment.

Reflecting on his time with Adele, he said remorsefully, "Some times it is just as illuminating to know what you don't have than what you do have."

"So, where do I go or what do I do to find the kind of love you felt for Adele?"

"Ah, lass, you can't plan it out. Adele fell in my lap, literally and figuratively. You just never know on the trip of life what lies beyond the next bend in the road."

"That is a bit scary."

"It also should be a bit exciting."

"Maybe, I should try a computer dating site."

"I doubt if you would be comfortable with that. But, you do what you think is best."

"I'll think about it. The best thing would be to have you cloned in a younger version."

"Flattering, but not what is for you. We are a good fit because we blend and bond through the ages. That is not the kind of romantic adventure you need and deserve."

"Why should love be so elusive?"

"Because, as I learned with Adele, it is an optimum. There are a host of feelings and sensations below that. The secret is not to confuse any of those with love, although as I now know that is easy to do."

"I am too anxious to be patient."

"There is much truth to the saying that you cannot rush love. Once you find it, it will stay in your mind and heart."

Those words had extra meaning for him, and it was not

surprising that the dreams he had that night were about Adele. The dreams seemed so real because the love was real. Tom would carry the significance and effects of that until his own death. It would be repeated and solidified in his dreams. A dream life can be it all if that is all you can have.

TWENTY-EIGHT

Adele's ashes were in a plain wooden box, just as she would probably have wanted it. Tom placed it on an empty shelf in the bookcase, a place of its own befitting the memories it carried with it. He sat in a chair and stared at it for a long time. Their love could have carried with it further satisfying times, and that might have produced a stronger will for her to live on. Yet, within his sorrow he could understand that she exercised her free will for what she felt was best all around. He would probably do something similar if he ever got to a point where he had an incurable condition accompanied by increasing pain so that there was a diminishing enjoyment of life and an increasing burden on a caretaker. The final decision is far from an easy one. At times, circumstances may dictate the direction of that personal will.

The next day was Mac's twenty-eighth birthday. Tom had already purchased the perfect gift – a large and beautifully enhanced photograph of a double rainbow that he had custom framed. He envisioned her hanging it in the office. The walls were barren, and besides being meaningful it would add a touch of color to the surroundings. It took two rolls of gift wrap to package it up so it would be a surprise. Mac loved it, and she hung it on the wall facing her desk so she could stare at it repeatedly. She gave Tommy an extra long and ardent hug.

The Cayman Islands investment investigation was wrapped up,

and the results were positive so the investor was pleased even with the probable shock of a hefty bill for the billable hours put in. Mac grinned accordingly.

Andrew telephoned Mac several times inviting her to dinner. She kept turning him down seeing no value in it. Tom suggested she accept to give the guy a chance to further apologize, and that was part and parcel of Tom's basic philosophy not to burn bridges behind you. So, on Andrew's fourth call Mac agreed to meet him at the Lonesome Duck.

Andrew was waiting for her at the restaurant. She was dressed more casually this time, the tailored white shirt tucked firmly into gray slacks. It brought admiring glances from him as well as other patrons.

Once seated at the table, he inquired, "You seem to be in great shape. Do you work out?"

"No, I don't. I get enough exercise as a detective."

"I don't get enough exercise. An undertaker is a sedentary form of life. I am planning on doing things differently in Asheville." He paused as the waitress filled the glasses with the wine he had ordered. "I thought a lot about you when I was away. I was going to wait until we finished eating, but I am too excited. I want to run an idea by you."

"I am listening."

"I would love to have you come with me to Asheville. I really like you and I think we can be good for each other. You can find detective work there I am sure."

Mac did not have to think long about that kind of suggestion. The delay in responding was due to the lesson Tommy imparted about not being unnecessarily cruel when you have to do or say something unpleasant. "Flattering and tempting, Andrew, but I can't leave my mother or Tommy. I do like you as a friend, but I am afraid it can be nothing more. I think you have made a good decision for yourself, and

I wish you success and happiness."

He was glum. "Instead of a kiss of affection, an undertaker can recognize a kiss of death. Even if I was not an undertaker I would recognize that."

They ate the meal mainly in silence. The thank you and the goodbye were cordial. Mac gave him a friendly hug, careful not to press her body to him. She was relieved, and was sure he would bounce back from any disappointment.

When she told Tommy all about it, his response was as she would have predicted it. "The beginning of a trail of broken hearts. Your own heart and mind will be a better guide than I can ever be."

"My mind and heart are perceptive because of your guidance."

"Then, for sure, the trail of broken hearts will lead to the pots of gold at the end of each of the double rainbows."

"I hope so."

TWENTY-NINE

April finally told the children about the temporary separation. She had run out of excuses when they had called and also asked to speak to Tom. While shocked and saddened by the news, marital life in the modern world is so filled with such developments they accepted the decision as one not made in haste and perhaps not irreparable.

Meanwhile, some new cases came into the office. One was from an elderly woman who wanted to find out where certain relatives were buried so that she could arrange to be buried close by. The few living relatives she contacted were unable to give her any information. Another was by a computer company going through a hiring phase, and they wanted Tom to check the veracity of certain resume assertions of leading candidates. A third case, prompted by a senior lady who had given a bunch of her deceased husband's items to an auction house to auction off for her, and now she wanted to retrieve two of the items since her son voiced a desire to have them to remember his father by. She had received an itemized listing of the sales but no buyer information. Tom was authorized to offer double the winning bid price for the return of the items.

Another interesting development was a telephone call to Mac from Gloria at the end of which Gloria asked to speak to Tom. "Tom, since Mac has spoken so highly of you and keeps telling me I can learn so much from you, I would like to treat you to lunch so I can see for myself."

"Gee, I don't think in all of my years I have been invited to lunch by a beautiful woman. There is probably a first for everything. I am not so much a fool to turn you down."

"Great. I have no funerals tomorrow. Will that work for you?"

"Sure."

"I'll pick you up at your office at 11:30."

"Fine. Where are we going?"

"It's a surprise."

"Even an old man likes surprises, pleasant ones that is."

When Gloria came to pick him up, she first hugged Mac and they talked for a few minutes. Tom was pleased to note the friendship developing there.

In the car, Gloria, who looked very attractive in a gray pants suit, asked, "Do you like seafood?"

He quipped, "As the saying goes, when I see food I like it."

"Good. I made a reservation at the Lighthouse. Ever been there?"

"Actually, no."

"It was once a real lighthouse that was converted to a restaurant years ago. The food is very good, although expensive. I want to treat you to the best so you will present to me your best."

"I was once a real man, now just a flaying senior."

"From what Mac tells me, you are as real as it gets."

"I have fooled her big time. Also, she does not want to insult her boss."

"I will make my own determination."

It was an enjoyable meal accompanied by scintillating conversation. Tom found Gloria to be bright, articulate, and reasonable in thought and action. She also hung on every word he uttered as if she was eager to pick his brain.

As they were finishing dessert, Gloria pronounced, "I have an additional reason for taking you to lunch."

Tom smiled. "I had a feeling that was the case. I was just wondering what has taken you so long. When one shoe drops, the other is bound to follow."

She cleared her throat. "Now that Andrew has broken out from the yoke, it makes me wonder about myself. It depresses me to think about running a mortuary for the rest of my life. I think I should seek out and try other things. I would like to volunteer to help in some of your cases. That concept intrigues me. I didn't really have a chance to get my feet wet in trying to track Andrew down."

"I think Mac may have exaggerated about what we do. She is so upbeat it colors her total outlook. It is as much drudgery as most other jobs, maybe even more at times. I will see what I can do, rather what you can do to get a taste of it."

"Thank you, kind man."

"No, thank you charming lady, with a special thanks for the lunch. Can I leave the tip, at least?"

"No. It is a complete treat, and has been that way for me as well."

"An apparent case of a double treat."

THIRTY

Back at the office, Tom and Mac drove to the Americana Auction House. It was located outside of the city on a rural road. An old barn had been modernized and converted to a place that could hold a bidding crowd. All kinds of items were strewn on the outside of the building as well as along the walls inside as they went through the open door.

Auctioneers are an odd lot. Part salesman, part comic, an auctioneer fosters a competitive atmosphere as he or she tries to present a jovial and entertaining event to put attendees in a bidding mood. It takes a certain personality type to fill the role, some more successful than others. It takes time and patience to build up a good reputation.

There did not seem to be anyone around. At the back of the building there was a counter and two desks behind it. It was not until they reached the counter did they see a man asleep with a cowboy hat pulled down over his face leaning back in a desk chair and with his feet up on the desk.

Tom coughed and the middle-aged man peered out from under the hat. "Hey, ole timer," his voice husky and loud, "Do you want to auction off that sweet young thing you have with you?"

Tom responded quickly, "To the contrary, she wants to auction me off as an antique."

"Won't bring much," the man said as he stood up, "Nobody

wants a useless item that is not even pretty to look at."

"Thank you very much. I already know that."

"What can I do for you folks?"

"I am Tom Lloyd, and I understand that Mrs. Feingold called to tell you I would be around."

"Ah, yes, the detective."

"Right on. This is my partner detective, Mac."

"I'll deal with her."

"Sorry, we are a package deal. Anyway, you know why we are here."

"Normally, we don't give out such information. But, Mrs. Feingold and her husband, when he was alive, are regulars so I make an exception. I am Brock Harpoon, better known as Captain Harpoon."

"Thanks, Captain. The two items are an Olympus watch and pair of wood carved bookends."

"Yup. I already pulled the records. Went to two different bidders – the watch to Deacon Filbert and the bookends to Wingate Blake. I'll write down the addresses and telephone numbers."

"You are a true captain," Tom offered.

"A true prince," Mac added which brought a broad smile to the auctioneer's face.

On the way back to the office, Tom spoke remorsefully. "You know, sweet thing, right now my heart is not in all this. I keep thinking of Adele, and the thoughts are melancholy. When the plug gets pulled on what all of a sudden was a life mission, everything else, at least for the moment, is secondary."

"I feel for you, Tommy," as she reached out her hand and put it on his.

"I had a wonderful dream about her last night. She will always be alive in my dreams."

Mac enfolded his hand with her fingers. "She is your angel."

"Yes, and so are you. And do you know who else has emerged as an angel – Gloria. She was in another dream, and symbolically behind her was a double rainbow. You are both my angels, and if my name was Charlie you would be Charlie's Angels. However, you have to settle to be Tom's Angels. Maybe, I'll just sit back and let my angels do the work."

"Tempting concept, Tommy."

"And, to begin, you select which bidder you want to tackle and I will have Gloria handle the other one."

"I'll go after Deacon. Gloria can get her feet wet with Wingate because he sounds too stuffy for me. Tom's Angels in full action!"

THIRTY-ONE

Mac telephoned Deacon Filbert the following morning. He was not at home, so she left a detailed message on his answering service and asked him to call her as soon as he could.

Deacon returned the call late in the afternoon when he came home from work. He explained that he liked the watch but was willing to return it if fully reimbursed. The winning bid was $64.00, and with the buyer's premium and the tax the total was $78.40. He suggested she come the next day to his workplace to get the watch if that worked for her. Since it did, he told her that he was a teacher at Bayville Elementary School and that she should come at 11:30 while he was on lunch break. Because of the tight security schools are forced to have these days, the school would be locked but he would clear her admission in advance and all she would have to do would be to show some identification. An office staffer would then take her to the lunchroom.

Deacon's greeting was friendly. He was short, maybe no more than an inch taller than she was, with thinning brown hair, and a bit on the hefty side. He had a pleasant face, wire glasses, and a warm smile. He was the only person in the lunchroom, explaining that the other teachers were on cafeteria duty. He invited her to sit at one of the tables. "I hope you don't mind if I eat while we talk as this is the only free time I have during the day. Would you like half of my sandwich, or I could get you some coffee?

"Kind of you, but I will be having lunch when I get back to my office."

He gave her the watch and she gave him the money. "That was the first auction that I had actually bought something. My daughter and I have gone a few times because it is fun to watch and hear the crowd and auctioneer, and my daughter just loves the hot dogs they have there. They pile all kinds of stuff on them."

"How old is she?"

"Seven going on fifteen. She is a student here at the school."

"Does your wife go with you?"

He hesitated for a moment, his voice a bit more somber. "She died nearly two years ago."

"I am so sorry."

"Thank you. It is especially hard for Shelby, my daughter. Death is not easy to accept at any age, but for a youngster it involves factors and feelings for them difficult to understand."

"Very true. I am just beginning to comprehend emotional pain."

"Emotional pain can last a long time, and it is constantly evolving."

"So I am aware."

"I try to be here for her all of the time, but she misses her mother."

"Emotional support can be a constant, no doubt, and it is probably not easy to balance giving too little or too much."

"For a child, as I can see from Shelby and the other students at the school, there is never a question of too much."

"It must be challenging to be a teacher."

"People have no clue. Especially in these trying times, teachers walk a bridge between challenges." He stared at her business card. "I imagine there are challenges in what you do."

"There are."

"What made you decide that you wanted to be a detective?"

"My boss, Tommy, is my mentor. His experience with life and his wisdom as an elder drew me to work with him. What led you to teaching?"

"It is good to have someone to look up to. I became interested in teaching because of the fascinating world of the child. They have an unending and unconfined curiosity, as well as an honest and genuine reaction to people and events, at least until society puts an unnecessary cap on it and steers them on a narrow path."

"You sound like a rebel."

"Always have been; always will be. I have been involved in many unpopular causes. I suppose that is part and parcel of the child still in me."

Mac liked the things he said and the way he said them. Even through his glasses she was sure she saw a burning light in his brown eyes. As Tommy often said she should expect the unexpected. One may not know or even guess what may lie just beyond the next bend on the road of life. "I think there is still some child left in me."

"How so?"

"I still get excited over new things, and my curiosity is easily aroused."

"Admirable features, I would say."

"At the same time I earnestly desire maturity, the kind Tommy has. He is so wise that I keep a journal of his sayings. There will come a day I will have to publish it as the fountain of all wisdom. He is part Confucius and part Ann Landers."

Deacon laughed, and it felt good to laugh. He was enchanted by this pretty and peppy detective. "Have you ever been to an auction?"

"No."

"My daughter and I are going on Saturday. Would you like to

join us? That is, if your husband or boy friend doesn't mind. After all, in a way you still owe me a watch so if one comes up at the auction you can bid on it on my number."

"There is no husband and no boy friend. I suppose now I have to watch for watches. I'd like to go. Will Shelby be upset?"

He chuckled. "You'll get to know the little viper. She loves all people, all animals, just about everything. I just have to warn you she talks incessantly."

"I can handle that. Her love for hot dogs might be contagious."

He smiled. "I am sure she will be excited to meet a lady detective."

"I hope so."

Driving back to the office, Mac had a pleasant sense about the meeting with Deacon. He was a person worth getting to know. He was interesting and polite, and his reactions and conversation appeared to be natural and unrestrained. She liked that.

"And, so a new chapter begins," Tom commented on the telling of the meeting with Deacon.

"How many chapters are there in the Book of Life?", Mac responded.

"Ah, one of the great unknowns. Even more puzzling, which and when is the final chapter? I may be on mine, but you have a long way to go."

"None of that fatalistic talk, boss. Anyway, your final chapter will be a final chapter for me as well."

"None of that kind of talk, lass. I will tell you a secret about two for the ages. I live in each chapter that you live even when my chapters run out. That is why there are two rainbows."

THIRTY-TWO

Gloria certainly was pleased that Tom was giving her a taste of detective life, even if the matter was less than exciting or glamorous. She was accustomed to being bogged down in dull routine matters in the funeral business. At least this would get her out and about. If Andrew could make a total break away from the family business, she was rightfully entitled to take some small tastes of different life styles. If a particular road became overly enticing, she would have to plan accordingly and the family would have to accept it just as little fuss was raised when Andrew made his big announcement.

The telephone number for Wingate Blake was for a law firm. When she called, she was told before her call was put through to him that Mr. Blake was an Associate with the firm. He was friendly enough, telling her that he liked handcrafted items and that the bookends were now in use on the bookcase in his office. Under the circumstances, he was willing to part with them, the total outlay he made for them was $87.15. He checked his calendar and said he was available the next day at 11:00 if she wanted to come and get them. That worked for her, and hopefully a quick successful resolution would prompt Tom to give her an expanded assignment.

When the receptionist led Gloria to Wingate's office in the plush surroundings Gloria was impressed by the place and the man himself. As he stood to greet her, she noticed he was taller than Andrew and with handsome rugged youthful features. His suit jacket was on the back of his chair, and a striped tie looked neat against the blue shirt. A fine specimen of a man she thought to herself.

Wingate's thoughts ran down a similar path. Appearing before him was a tall and beautiful woman, and it was enticing to know that a detective could be so attractive. "Have a seat, Miss Nathan." She sat in the chair before his desk and then he sat.

"Very nice office you have here, Mr. Blake."

"Please call me Wingate or Win as most people do. The office and surroundings are show for clients."

"Works for me, Win. You can call me Gloria."

"The bookends are on the table behind you. I have already taken them off the bookshelf. I go to the auction every once and awhile because I collect handcrafted wooden items, and you just never know what may come up at an auction where a bargain can be found. These really caught my fancy, but I don't mind surrendering them under the circumstances."

She pulled an envelope out from her handbag. "Here is the payment in full. I guess in your world and mine we would have a common term... case closed."

He smiled. "Neither one of us probably has closed a case so fast."

"This is my first case."

"Really?"

"I am just helping out at the Agency. I am actually a mortician."

"You're kidding!"

"No. I am Gloria Nathan of the R. Nathan & Sons Funeral Home."

Another broad smile. "Listen, lady, you can have the bookends but not my body."

Thinking to herself that she would like the body, she gushed, "I don't deal with live ones."

"You sure are full of surprises."

"I catch them off guard that way."

"Same ploy I would use in court."

"Have you been a lawyer for a long time?"

"Not really. I graduated from law school three years ago, passed the bar, and have been an Associate here for nearly two years. I do not actually get to court much as the firm deals mainly with commercial matters which is more negotiations and paper work. If you don't mind me asking, how come you are in that business as you don't appear to be one of the sons."

She laughed. "Long standing family business. My father is one of the sons, now retired, and my brother and I run the day-to-day."

"I have an idea. I am about to go to lunch, will you join me?"

"Won't your wife be jealous?"

"No wife."

"Girl friend?"

"A few around, but nothing serious. Are you taken?"

She was going to say yes by you, but stifled the impulse. "A corpse is good for only one date."

They dined at a small cafe across the street from the building the law firm was in. Conversation was easy, and it was obvious they both were enjoying the company. Wingate was from an old Savannah, Georgia family, that city not far from Hilton Head. His parents were still living there, and he had two younger sisters who were now both in advanced college programs. He had a small house not from the law firm and close to the harbor where he kept a boat. When he was not occupied with work or the boat, he went to Savannah for the weekends. He invited her to go out on the boat Saturday or Sunday, but she had to turn him down because she had funerals both days. It was arranged for the following Saturday.

Mac knew something good had happened when Gloria came back to the office carrying the bookends and with a glow on her face. She had not had a chance to tell Gloria about Deacon. They exchanged the romantically inclined stories, and all that Tom could do was to grin and bear it. Tom's Angels were in full active mode. Perhaps, the Americana Auction House was a dating service in disguise.

THIRTY-THREE

On Saturday, after Mac left to meet Deacon and Shelby at the auction, Tom took down the box containing Adele's ashes and put it on the dining room table. He stared at it for an extended period, the longing in his heart increasing with the time. He relived in his mind some of the enchanting moments from the wedding weekend. To find love and then to lose it so soon after is a cruel fate.

Sitting at the table, he stretched out his hand to grasp the box as if he was reaching out to hold her. As he did so, he looked at the three-inch scar above his thumb which was the result of a cut he received as a boy and which served as a constant reminder of an incident in his life. He now had a scar in his heart as well.

It was one thing to live with a memory, it was another as to what to do about it. As Adele would always be a presence in what remained of his life, he would have to put that presence to good use. As he touched the box, it was as if Adele was speaking to him. My love, help others as you helped me.

He should have thought of it sooner. He telephoned Florence at the nursing home and told her that he would like to start visiting with those there who were the loneliest, those that had no family or friends and who did not have any visitors. Florence told him that there were a number of people like that and she commended him on what she thought was a wonderful idea.

It was after lunch when Tom arrived at the nursing home. He

met with Florence first, and she arranged a visit for him with Ellen Markham. Ellen had been in the home for over seven years, and was now gradually slipping away with an assortment of ailments. She had no family, and as far as Florence could remember never had a visitor. She told Tom that Ellen still had her mental faculties.

Tom met Ellen, who was in a wheelchair, in the TV room. She was a small, frail woman with stringy gray hair tousled down over wire glasses upon a weathered face. Since it was a nice day, he pushed the wheelchair so they could chat on the porch where he sat in a chair by her.

"Are you comfortable, Ellen?"

Her voice was weak and raspy. "Yes, thank you. Thank you for visiting with me. There is nobody who comes to see me."

"I am happy to do it. I was close to Adele Scheinfeld who was here. Did you know her?"

Ellen's eyes were nearly shut and Tom was not sure she heard him or was even awake. "Yes, I did. She died. I will join her soon."

"I am here to cheer you up. No talk about dying. Tell me about yourself. As you can see, I am also an old timer so we can share secrets."

A hint of a smile on taut lips. "My secrets die with me."

"Sharing a secret is a meaningful moment."

"Tell me your secret."

"Ah, fair damsel, I have already told you my best secret. I loved Adele. That love now extends to all who knew her or who need love."

"That is a nice secret. My secret haunts my soul. Maybe, I will tell you if I can trust you. Can you be trusted?"

"You will have to make that determination yourself. Tell me about you."

"A boring story for a stranger to hear. My husband and I ran a small convenience store near here. We worked long hours every day. Never enjoyed it, and never made much money. One night he had a heart attack and was gone. I couldn't handle the store by myself and couldn't afford to hire anyone so I sold it just as I was falling ill with bad results, and the sale money went to the home. And, here I am, just an old woman waiting to die. No relatives, no friends. One secret I will tell you. I am not afraid to die. I am afraid to live."

Tom reached out and grasped a cold and wrinkled hand. He was not sure if she was aware of it as she had fallen asleep. He sat next to her and held her hand for almost an hour. She awakened with a slight, knowing smile on those crusty lips. He wheeled her to her room and promised he would visit her the next Saturday. He sealed the promise with a hug.

He had time for one more visit. Olivia Woodward, bed-ridden and terminal, was the longest resident at the home. She was a large black woman who occupied nearly the entire bed. Florence said she was feisty and cantankerous, and she was not sure she had all of her faculties. She told Tom he would find out for himself. Olivia claimed to forget everything, but Florence was not sure if that was true or just an act.

Olivia was propped up on the bed as Florence introduced Tom to her and then she left. Olivia peered at him from under heavy eyelids. Her voice boomed out at him. "Hey, white boy, you the new kid on the block?"

Tom laughed. "No kid, and no new. I am here to visit with you."

"Do I know you?"

"No. Would you like to know me?"

She looked beyond him as if he had brought others with him. "Are you worth knowing, white boy?"

"Not the boy in me which ran away from me a long time ago,

but the man in me is awfully friendly."

"Don't know what friendly is or what it can do for me."

"Care to find out?"

She nodded and he sat in the chair by the bed. He told her about him, and then she seemed anxious to talk about herself. She was the youngest of six children, all from the same mother and with an assortment of fathers. The mother and the others were all gone now. The family had nothing and struggled all of the time. Only State funding provided a place in the home for her when she became incapacitated. Now, she was waiting to get into Heaven because it had to be better there than here.

"If you could," he asked in earnest, "Do one thing, what would it be?"

"I'd have to think on that for a spell."

"Before I go, I would like to make as many friends as I can. That is why I am here. I want to be your friend."

"Pearly words, white boy, but what's in it for you?"

"Makes me feel good, and I bet it would make you feel good, too."

"Would you feel bad when I die?"

"Real bad."

"Ain't sure I ever had a friend."

"It's not too late."

"And, if I don't want to be your friend?"

"I'll still be yours."

"And if I tell you I don't like white boys?"

"I'll tell you I love black women."

"Ever kiss one?"

"Actually, yes. I have almost forgotten it, but when I was a boy in New York there was a black family down the street. They had a daughter who went to my school. One day we walked home together,

She asked me if I had ever kissed a girl on the lips. I told her I hadn't, and she confided in me that she hadn't either but was hankering to try it. I wasn't sure about it, and really had not thought much about such things, but she grabbed me by the hand and lead me into an alley. Behind some garbage cans piled high on each other she leaned into me and pulled me close to her. We kissed, and it was really something. I dreamed about it for a long time after that, and hoped we could do it again. It seemed as if we were never alone after that."

Olivia grimaced from pain. "Sounds like a made up story to me."

"It happened, for sure."

"If you want to be my friend, you have to kiss me. Up to that, white boy?"

He stood up, leaned real close to her face and planted a smooch on the thick lips well aware of the strong medicinal taste. Her first smile. "Now, we are friends."

THIRTY-FOUR

Saturday was a very enjoyable day for Mac. Deacon and Shelby were waiting at the entrance to the auction house. Shelby was a delightful youngster and true to form. She talked a great deal, although it was not just rambling but was a series of a young girl's observations and reactions to things around her. She talked much about her father and some sad references to her mother.

As the day wore on Mac felt even more at ease in their company. She was herself, laughing and commenting without hesitation or having to be aware of what she was saying. That was a meaningful moment.

Even when they took a break from the entertaining bidding process to have hot dogs, it was a happy time. She and Shelby laughed when Deacon dribbled mustard down his chin.

No watch came up for the bidding. Mac was well aware of Deacon glancing sideways at her often and she felt he was as interested in her as she was in him. The father and daughter togetherness generated a warmth in her heart that she was not accustomed to, although it was certainly welcome. Sustainability was the looming factor.

When the auction ended and they went out to the parking lot, both Deacon and Shelby hugged her. Deacon invited her over for a barbeque at their house the next day.

Tommy was not at the apartment when Mac returned. His note read that he went out on an adventure. She started to prepare dinner and just knew that there would be a lively conversation at the dinner table.

Tom. exhausted, slumped into an easy chair when he arrived at the apartment. "Ah, lass, what a day!"

Mac came over and kissed him on the cheek. "Even an old man can have a tiring adventure. Wait until you hear about the romantic trip your favorite assistant had."

"Sounds like the two for the ages have found the pots of gold at the end of the rainbows."

"Could very well be. Dinner is just about ready. We'll talk between chewing."

"Sounds like there will be all sorts of things to digest."

The eating turned out to be secondary to the relating of the day's activities. Mac told her story first, detailing impressions of father and daughter while emphasizing how natural it all was and how comfortable she had been.

Tom reached across the table and patted her hand. "I am happy for you. Just don't rush to judgment. The trip can be and should be as important as the destination."

"Another journal entry, Tommy."

"I'll be watching in more ways than one."

"Ha."

Tom related in detail his visit to the home, including the infamous Olivia kiss. Mac was attentive and smiling. "Wow, Tommy, I think you have found a reason and an outlet for your passion. I have never kissed a black man. Of course, I really have kissed very few men, period. Will you go back next weekend?"

"Hope to."

"What is Florence like? Anything close to Adele?"

"She is nice enough, although I think she is more business-oriented. She does have a genuine interest in the folks there. She is married, but he does not seem to be involved with the home."

They were tired so went to bed early. Tom was anxious to see where his dreams would take him. He was not disappointed. There were glimpses of detailed events with Adele, April, Ellen, and Olivia. Just as he would get immersed in a particular event Mac would pull him back toward the double rainbow behind her. He figured she was assuming the role of a daughter pulling him away from danger and acting as the steadying influence in his life.

THIRTY-FIVE

When Tom called April to inform her of his latest attempt to help people, she was aghast. "Each thing you do is crazier than the one before it. Those people have all sorts of diseases, many contagious I bet, and you are purposely exposing yourself." How could one not think that such an action was at the very least noble? He miscalculated that about her just as he had other things. He shook his head in disbelief. The rift between them had become a chasm.

Mac had a wonderful time on Sunday. Deacon's house, a bit smaller than most others in the tidy neighborhood, was attractive and well kept. He tended to gardens in the front and back of the house, including an herb garden that was used for cooking. Shelby enjoyed showing her around, particularly her room which was filled with all sorts of objects, most of which had a story to be related.

At one point when they were alone in the kitchen, Deacon took hold of her hand. "Since Cindy died I have had no interest in romance until I met you. You sure have caught my fancy. Even Shelby talks about you a lot. You are one captivating detective."

She squeezed his hand. "Nice to know you have a fancy. You have captured my fancy as well. Maybe our fancies can meet halfway."

He laughed, and it felt good to laugh. There had been too much sadness in the house. "I have a feeling that wherever we are it's midway."

She leaned in close to him and they kissed briefly. "An extra dessert," she whispered.

"As sweet as it gets."

Driving back to the apartment at the end of the day Mac decided she was in love. This had to be love she thought to herself. She was sure Tommy would have some input, but she could not deny the warm and tender sentiment she had towards Deacon and Shelby. She had not considered finding an already built family to smooth out the rough edges of the challenges confronting her growth and pursuit of a life, but here it was potentially there for her to latch onto. She was not rushing to judgment as Tommy had advised not to do. It was more of a finding and a desire to hold it and build upon it. It was an opportunity, and she very much wanted to take advantage of it. There had been few opportunities in her life, and as with the discovery of Tommy and his interests that she was now a desired part of, it was fortuitous to be in the right place at the right time.

"I am happy for you," Tommy uttered as he hugged her warmly. "Sooner is better than later. I was planning to emphasize the possibility that your desired discovery might be a long haul and debating with myself how to prepare you for that. It is unnecessary now. Just be certain of the feelings and expectations of others after you confirm such at your own end."

"You do know that this in no way affects or diminishes the love I feel for you?"

"I know that. There is more than one kind of love, and there can be special loves held by special people. Your heart is big enough to accommodate it all. I knew that from the beginning, and I think you know it now as well."

"You better believe it."

Tom told Mac about April's reaction to his news. "I suppose we are world's apart."

Mac hugged him. "Don't let it sway you. Adele approves, and I approve."

"That's the best seal of approval."

THIRTY-SIX

New cases kept coming in which kept them involved along with the old ones. The enterprise was quickly becoming profitable. Mac took a day trip to a cemetery near Columbia, South Carolina to check on interred relatives for the client seeking that. Even as busy as they had become, Tom's thoughts rested with Adele and the folks at the home. He was anxious to do more there. His mission in life had changed, and against all advice as a bad maneuver he was changing horses in midstream.

Being anxious for the weekend to arrive made the week drag on. Tom left for the home right after Mac left to spend the day with Deacon and Shelby.

Florence had already wheeled Ellen to the porch awaiting Tom's arrival on the warm and clear day. Ellen had doubts as to the promised visit, but was glad to see Tom show up.

"Good morning, Ellen. I told you I would be back."

"I am surprised you came back. I don't know why."

"Here's why." He gave her a big hug.

"I have no money to leave you in my will."

"Your presence is all the present I need. We are here together on a beautiful day to spend a pleasant time. We can prove to each other that we are still alive and kicking, still functioning, and looking forward to tomorrow. Today is our journey to tomorrow."

"I must admit you are one happy old man."

"A happy old man that is going to make an old lady happy."

"That would be a miracle."

"Each and every breath we take is a miracle."

"I'm on to you."

"You are?"

"Yup. You are trying to make me believe I can trust you so I'll tell you my secret."

"Way off, sweetheart. Secret or no secret, you are my kind of woman."

"Well, all of your sweet talk won't help you one little bit. I can't trust flowery talk. Where's the man in you?"

"Good question. What you see is what you get. I am me and only me." He completely believed what he was saying. "If it is not good enough, so be it. I am the cake with no icing. Easy to swallow and easy to digest."

"I'm not fond of cake."

"That's alright. I will keep the cake. You just be fond of me."

They talked for more than an hour. He told her stories about the law practice, the detective agency, and Mac. She related incidents that she remembered from running the convenience store, including the one time they were held up by a robber who actually apologized for doing so explaining that it was the only way he could get money to feed his family. Tom wheeled Ellen back to her room when she confessed she was tired.

Tom received a boisterous greeting from Olivia when he entered her room. "Just what I need," her voice booming defying her tenuous medical condition, "Another white boy. A white boy come to see me last week and I throwed him out."

"Well, he is back for more punishment."

"You ain't him. He was good looking."

"See what happens when I age a week. I'll prove to you it's me."

"How so, white boy?"

"Pucker up, baby, I am coming in for a landing." He kissed those heavy lips and watched as they spread into a broad smile.

"If I had any idea white boys could kiss like that I would've had my share when the going was good."

"It is never too late to make up for lost time." He firmly believed that himself.

"Too bad white boys are dumb. I knows it is too late, way too late."

Olivia lay back and was quiet for a few minutes. He surmised she was battling her pain. Her voice softened and she started to tell him things from her past as if he knew the people she mentioned and the places she referred to. Stories were unfinished, and the sentiments described were cryptic. Facts were hurled out in whatever order they came to her mind. All of a sudden she yelled, "Get out, white boy. My pain is bad, real bad. I gotta be alone."

Florence took Tom to the dining room so he could be with those residents amble enough to eat meals there. She particularly wanted Tom to meet Leon Mandroll, who she described as a crabby old buzzard who never had a kind word for anyone or about anything. Leon had been in the home for several years with an assortment of ailments. He did not get visitors or receive any mail.

Florence sat at the table with Tom and Leon, as well as one other lady, Constance Green, who was deaf so impervious to Leon's argumentative ramblings. Tom tried several times to initiate a conversation with Leon, but Leon ignored him.

As they were finishing the dessert, Leon turned to Tom and snapped at him, "Don't waste your friendly gestures on me. They don't work, and I am not interested."

Feigning surprise, Tom urged, "Now, now, everyone can use a friend."

"Not me. What for?"

"To share a laugh or a tear."

"I don't laugh or cry. Nothing to laugh at and certainly nothing worth crying over."

"Then I make up for both of us. I find multiple things to laugh at or cry about each day. It's the full expanse of human behavior and one need only to look around to find multiple things or people to laugh at or cry about."

"Hogwash! Florence put you up to this, didn't she?"

"Leave me out of this," Florence interjected as she got up and led Constance out of the room.

It was just Tom and Leon at the table. Tom asked the server for another cup of coffee. "You think you are a tough nut to crack, don't you, Leon?"

"I am, and proud of it."

"Well, I am as stubborn as you are. Did you know Adele Scheinfeld?"

Leon was quiet for a moment. "Yeah. A nice lady who never bothered me."

"I was in love with her. I cry over her death every day. In her way, she has asked me to make friends with everyone here."

"Dead people don't talk."

"Oh, yes they do, and they have plenty to say. Especially when they feel there are people who need to hear what they have to say."

"You are wasting your breath."

"Were you married?"

"Nope."

"Did you ever have a friend, even as a boy?"

"Nope."

"I don't believe that."

"Well, if I did, I have long since forgotten it."

"What was your occupation?"

"I was a mail carrier."

"Did you get to know the people on your route?"

"Some."

Tom continued with what he had to consider a cross examination. "Did you talk to them, have an interest in them?"

"Some."

"I was a lawyer, and now I run a detective agency for seniors."

"What has that to do with me?"

"Maybe, I will take you on as a client and try to find out why you are such a hard ass."

Leon laughed, at least it was a slight chuckle. "You're a funny guy."

"Friendly, too, if you give me a chance."

"No way," Leon got up and walked out of the room leaving Tom with an unfinished cup of coffee.

Florence took Tom to meet Delores Huegnot, who was sitting in the little library alcove of the home. Delores had been in the home for a little over a year, was terminal, had no visitors, and despite a strong antidepressant medication along with a host of other medications, was extremely despondent.

After being introduced, Tom asked, "Would you mind if I sit with you for awhile?"

Delores looked at him with a blank stare, "It's a free country."

Delores probably was a pretty woman when young. Her features, now shriveled and crusty, were well proportioned. Even the remaining thin gray hair framed a perfectly oval face. Tom could imagine the now overly thin body probably caused from meager eating was most likely full and would have been fetching in form-fitting clothing. Too bad older people cannot remember the glory days of the past and the allures they possessed in a young life.

After a few minutes, Tom spoke wistfully, "I love books. Libraries are one of the most rewarding and peaceful places on Earth."

She turned to him and stared as if she was seeing him for the first time, "Books are the vessels that ably transfer us through life."

"I bet you were a librarian. Am I right?" Of course, Florence had told him that Delores had been a librarian for over forty years.

She just kept staring at him. "I was until they forced me to retire."

"Who is they?"

"The Devil and his disciples."

"But, they did not win."

"Yes, they did. Just look at what is left of me."

"You may be old, just as I am, but you still have books, still have life."

"You know nothing. Old is not life. These books are as old and as cold as I am. Nobody cares about them or even looks at them. If it is not something on TV or their phone, they're not interested."

"Who cares? You make your own way. Haven't you done that your entire life?"

She was silent although he could see a slight trembling of her body. "How do you know that?"

"Because I have done that, and I think we are the same."

"How come you are not in here?"

"Because I am not finished out there."

"I am dying."

"I know, but you do not have to be alone."

"Why are you talking to me?"

"I want to be your friend. I want to share your thoughts and feelings. I want to love you."

"Why me?"

"Because I think you want that."

"Nobody ever loved me, so I don't know what it is like."

"Do you want to find out?"

She hesitated. "No."

"Why not?"

"What good would it do me?"

"It would be good for me and we can enjoy it together."

"You make no sense."

"Since when do old folks have to make sense? It can be like a book, like a fairy tale. I can visit you every week. We can talk, we can laugh, we can cry. Most importantly, we can hug. I would like to hug you. May I?"

She did not respond. He leaned over to her and hugged her carefully, well aware of a body barely there. When he drew back, a tear drop descended through the slit of one of Delores' eyes.

THIRTY-SEVEN

Mac was spending the weekend with the Filbert family, a place that was now repeatedly calling to her heart. It was also the Saturday that Gloria had arranged to go out on Win's boat. Those two already had an initial mutual attraction, and a carefree day of sun, water, and boating further enhanced the amorous feelings.

When Gloria emerged from below deck after she had changed from street clothes to a swim suit. Win was overtaken by an image of a statuesque beauty. Yet, it was more than a physical attraction. Throughout the day, there was an assortment of intellectual probings, exchanges of various thoughts, and a sharing of desired aspirations. Win was convinced that Gloria was a deep and interesting thinker, and her wit and expressions kept him fully involved as no other woman had challenged him before.

For Gloria, Win seemed to be everything she dreamed about as a man for her. It was easy for her to visualize being with him permanently. It was probably the last thing she had imagined when she went to retrieve a pair of bookends that she would wind up being in love. Yet, she could almost hear Tom urging that the best can happen when you least expect it.

Gloria was careful not to get too much sun. The funeral business kept her indoors most of the time and her fair skin was not used to long bouts of sun. She ran early in the morning before the sun gained its strength. It was comforting to find out that Win was also an early morning runner.

They ate the delicious picnic lunch that Win had brought onto the boat under a canopy that Win concocted so that she would be in the shade. After lunch there was an extended and meaningful embrace, both acknowledging that serious potential was in the air.

It was late when Gloria drove home from the harbor. It had been a long day although a wonderful one. She was not the least bit tired, as her heart and mind spinned with reliving the moments of the day. She was sure she had found the man of her dreams, and all of the usual visions entered into her mind of a family and future years spent together. It would also be the impetus to break away from the funeral business, and she decided she would ask Tom for a chance to become a detective at the agency. Tom had been joking when he referred to Tom's Angels, but Gloria really liked that idea. Finding a kind way to break such news to her father might be a problem. She did not want to hurt him or disappoint him, although he would have to accept that she had a life of her own to make. Adding that she had found a serious love interest might ease the way. Anyway, she was excited and looking forward to telling Mac about it all.

THIRTY-EIGHT

Tom's dreams had become erratic, probably because of the rush of various compelling emotions entering and attempting to control the nature and direction of his life. The only consistent presence was Mac and the double rainbow.

Florence telephoned to tell him that Olivia had died. Tom was troubled that he should have been there to hold her hand at death. Florence also added that Leon was asking about him and had urged that Tom visit with him first on Saturday.

On Saturday, Florence took Tom directly to Leon's room. Leon was sitting in a rocking chair and he motioned for Tom to sit in a chair that was next to him. "I was hoping you would show up," Leon quipped trying to sound indifferent.

Before answering, Tom looked around the room noticing that it was barren of any personal items. There were no pictures, and no items to reflect a personal preference or outlook. "How come?"

"I wanted to see if you are really a funny guy."

"Probably, not too funny today."

"Don't disappoint me."

"Life is full of sobering moments. I had one this morning when I got out of bed."

"What happened?"

"I went to the bathroom and saw an old man in the mirror who I did not recognize. He was looking back at me and asked 'Who are you?' I couldn't answer because I did not know who I was or even who I am. Sure, I know my name and why I was standing there, but I did not know who I really was. I have gone through a dramatic transition recently. I discovered the love of a lifetime with Adele, and it was gone with her death. It also brought on the realization that I have never really loved the woman I have been married to for many years. I had equated being comfortable with a woman as being in love with her. There is the staggering reality that I have, in effect, wasted all of those years. Then, I have become involved in the lives of some of the people here, people who apparently have nobody interested in them. One of them died this week. She died alone. I could have and should have been with her. So, when the man in the mirror asked me who I am, I could not answer."

Leon was quiet. He, too, was going through an introspection that he had avoided for such a long time. "I never planned to bare my soul. Now, I think I need to, just as you have privileged me by telling me your inner thoughts. I have lived most of my life in a self-imposed shell because I am a criminal in my own heart and mind. Early in my life because of cruel and thoughtless acts towards another I caused a tragic result that not even God could forgive me for. I will spare you the details even though I live them in my nightmares and in the dark recesses of my days. When I was a young man, I met a very sensitive woman who was a professional dancer. For reasons I do not know and could not accept, she loved me. Love is not even a strong enough word to describe it. She worshiped me. Most men would be ecstatic if that happened to them. For reasons that defy sense or logic, I cruelly and forcefully rejected her." Leon suddenly was silent and Tom was not sure he would hear any more, and could scarcely believe that this man was the same disinterested person he confronted the week before. Leon sobbed and his body shook so hard Tom thought he might fall out of the rocker. "Because of my extreme rejection she turned to drugs, and that in turn caused a serious accident leaving her crippled and then to a painful death. I have never gotten over it, and the coward in me has always stopped me from killing myself. I have suffered a thousand deaths. My punishment is to never be happy, never seek any form of pleasure, and to endure hardships that I deserve. I hate the world because I hate me."

Tom watched as Leon turned to stare out of the window, perhaps looking for the anguish that only he could see. Guilt is a heavy burden. "I don't know what to say. There is probably nothing I can say. Each of us has demons we need to deal with on our own terms."

"I don't expect or even want you to say anything. I never thought I would tell this to anyone. Telling it does not make me feel any better. I have no right to ask a favor from you, but I would like you to do something for me."

Tom had a premonition that he would be sorry for asking this. "What is that?"

"For the beautiful life I took, I would like you to execute me."

"I can't do that."

"You have to admit I deserve it."

"I cannot and will not judge somebody else. As I told you, I can't even be reasonable about myself."

"Think about it, please."

Would it be right to kill someone who cannot do it themselves for what they did that caused another to commit suicide? "I will."

Florence had already wheeled Ellen out to the porch to wait for Tom's visit. On the way, he passed Olivia's room. The door was closed, and there was a picture of Olivia and a red rose tacked to the door. A tear formed in his eye, and he was sure he had an irreparable hole in his heart. Yes, there are far too many things in this world to cry over.

Tom hugged Ellen. "It is almost lunch time."

"You are good at telling time."

"I know it is a happy time when I am with you. It's our enjoyable and captivating journey to tomorrow."

"There goes that sweet talk again. I like hearing it, but it means nothing. I still don't trust you."

"And I trust you and love you. Have we narrowed the gap even a little?"

"A little, maybe. Not enough to tell you a secret that would shake you to your boots."

"I will tell you what. Let me take you to the dining room so we can have a lover's lunch, and then we'll talk about it some more."

They had a quiet lunch, just the two of them at a small table. Ellen did most of the talking, relating more incidents in her life at the convenience store which had consumed so much of her existence. Then they went back out to the porch.

"I won't last long," Ellen urged as they settled down. "I usually take a nap after lunch."

"I will take you to your room whenever you say."

She chuckled. "I sleep alone."

"Shucks."

"Nice try, Romeo."

"You already know me real well. Still can't trust me?"

"Not for a secret that big. If I told you, you would be busting out to tell the world. Can't let that happen."

"Shucks, again."

"I am tired. Please, take me to my room."

He took her there, helped her onto the bed, and within a minute she was fast asleep. His curiosity sure was aroused about her secret, although he had a notion it would never get revealed. Whatever it was, it was big to her although it might just be something that has a personal significance which makes it loom large. Perhaps, just as he should not have asked Leon about the favor he was probably better off not knowing Ellen's secret. Especially, if it was something that he had to take action about.

Delores was in the library alcove. Tom knew that is where he would find her. He figured that was her safe spot. Many people have a comfort zone, an area in which they feel most at ease and protected. A particular place in that zone he called a safe spot, the favorite portion of the comfort zone. Surrounded by books would have to be that place for her. Books do not complain and books do not talk back.

He hugged her. "I'm back."

"I see."

"Any action on the books?"

"Why do you waste your time with me?"

"If I thought I was wasting my time, I would not be here. The more friends I have the better I feel. I hope it is the same for you."

"I don't need or want friends. They get in the way of dying."

"Precisely, I don't want you to die and I want to make your living time happy."

"Why?"

"We went through this last time. I love you and we can spend some time making each other happy."

"Suit yourself, but it won't work."

"You don't want a visitor?"

"No."

"You don't want someone to love you?"

"No."

"Why?"

"Because nobody ever did. Why start now?"

"Now is all there is."

Tom started to tell her all about himself and especially about Mac who he considers his daughter. He also told her about finding the abiding love with Adele, who Delores had known.

"I don't know if I feel more sorry for you or myself," Delores stated when he finished. She then told him about her barren life as a librarian in a place where she was ignored and unappreciated. She ended with a seething exclamation. "I would have killed them all if I could. When I die, I suppose they die with me." She stood, and to Tom's surprise she came up to him and hugged him and walked away.

THIRTY-NINE

Mac was in such a good mood Sunday evening when she returned to the apartment that Tom did not want to spoil it. She related animated stories about Deacon and Shelby. He waited until Monday to tell her about Leon's unusual request.

"Wow!," Mac exclaimed. "I thought the decision you had to make about going off with Adele for the wedding weekend was a toughie. This one is over the top."

"Not really. There is no way I would or could do it. I am not able to even consider taking the life of someone. That is contrary to a lifetime of established principles and morals. The problem is, how do I handle it?"

"Tell him what you just told me. He will understand that and will just have to accept it."

"Maybe, not that easy. Now that he has expressed outright such an idea, and was willing to approach me about it, I don't want him to try it with someone else."

"Tommy, I'm not sure you can control that."

"I need to try."

"Is he at all religious? Perhaps a clergyman can be persuasive."

"I doubt if he is. He has lived a lifetime in emotional isolation and self-punishment."

"Anything I can do?"

"Just being able to confide in you is your greatest

contribution."

"I am here for you with whatever and forever."

"Likewise."

"Did Ellen tell you her secret?"

"Not yet."

"Are you sure there is one? Maybe, she is being a lady of mystery as a way to keep you interested in her."

"Could be, although I doubt it. I think she would not care a bit if I didn't visit her again. There is a secret I am sure, but its nature is problematical. It may be big only in her eyes. She is very guarded about it, so it is important to her."

"Would it help if I visited with her?"

"She knows about you, but no sense getting you involved unless you really want to or there is a special need for you to be there."

"You know I will do whatever will help you?"

"I know that, sweetie, and I love you just that much more for it."

"Two rainbows are stronger than one.'

"Nobody can dispute that."

"What about Delores?"

"She's down on the world and everyone in it, especially herself. I may never be able to cheer her up or have her believe the significance of the journey to tomorrow. I will keep trying. The daunting situation is that there seem to be a host of folks there who could use support and direction. I wish I was a younger man with as much energy as determination."

"Nothing impedes my hero."

"I thought your hero is now Deacon?"

"He is a subhero."

"You are serious about him, aren't you?"

"From all I have learned from you this appears to be it for me, and I might add happily so."

"I might lose a roommate."

"A roommate maybe, but never a daughter. Your essence goes with me wherever I go."

"Nice to know."

When Tom got in the bed tired from a long day, the thinker in him prevented him from falling asleep. In addition to how best to handle Leon, since Mac talked about Ellen's secret, the vast and seemingly bottomless subject of a secret kept him alert. What is the true nature and essence of a secret? When does a secret stop being a secret? If it involves only one person and that person is deceased, if the divulging of it does not tarnish the person's image or hurt another what would be the reason for keeping a silence? Might it be just a matter of principle? If, over time, the context or significance of the secret has diminished, does that make a difference? Then, what if the secret is not about a real person or situation? What if Tom had a secret about the time he was with the insurance company, a fact which he is not sure ever happened, does that affect the character of the so-called secret? Does a secret remain a secret when told to someone else even with a pledge of confidentiality? Once opened up, the keeper of the secret has lost actual control of it. To what degree might the sensitivity of the person to whom a secret is told affect the revelation? Is there a secret about secrets?

FORTY

Tom did not need Florence to take him to the folks he wanted to see. He was familiar with the home now, and she had given him permission to do his visiting as he saw fit. She had that much confidence in his motives and ability to help.

Tom was anxious to settle the matter with Leon, so he went to see him first. He was not in his room, and Tom found out that he had gone for a walk. Tom found him sitting on a bench down a path from the home.

Tom sat down next to him on the bench. "You are out early."

It was an awkward moment before Leon responded. "The place can be very confining. At least, if I scream here nobody will hear me."

"What would you scream about?"

"So I could be set free."

"You don't like it in the home?"

"It's alright. It is a means to an end. Are you going to do what I asked?"

"No. And you know I wouldn't. Nobody would do such a thing. It is plain wrong. Plus, it would not be right for you. You have already punished yourself long and hard enough. Yes, it was a terrible chapter in your life, but have you ever considered that the true way to atone for that event is to help others? By helping even just one person avoid a tragic ending you will have made up for it."

"I don't see it that way."

"Isn't it worth a try?"

"I don't want to try. I want to end my suffering."

"I can't help you the way you think is easy. It is not. Don't put anyone in a position where they would be committing murder."

"How can it be murder when it is justified?"

"To you, perhaps, but not to society."

"That's the lawyer in you speaking. What does the man think?"

"One in the same. It is just plain wrong."

"You sure do speak your mind."

"I've been known to do that."

"Nothing I can say would convince you otherwise?"

"No, so let's now talk about living."

"Too late for me."

"Not too late, and certainly not too late to do something good for another."

"Like what?"

Tom thought for a moment. "Do you know Delores Huegnot?"

"I know who she is. Never spoke to her, never cared to or even thought about it. What about her?"

"She is terminal and extremely depressed. She used to be a librarian and books are her passion. She usually sits in the library alcove, and you would make a big inroad in her world if you just went there and told her you would like to take a book to your room to read and ask her guidance in selecting one."

"Why do I want to do that?"

"Because it will be doing something good for someone else, and perhaps along the way it may make you feel good about yourself."

"Impossible."

"You won't know unless you try it."

Leon grew silent. "I will think about it."

"Good."

Tom went to Ellen's room. There was a hint of a smile on her face when he hugged her. She nodded approval when he asked her if she wanted to go to the porch for awhile and then to have lunch with him.

Once on the porch, Ellen was anxious to talk. "It is nice to have you visit before I die."

"No talk about dying."

"That is all there is for me."

"Then, who would I visit?"

"There are plenty of others here who would listen to your sweet talk."

"But how many others have a secret?"

"Ah, so that is your reason after all. You just want to know my secret."

"Actually, no. I am trying to make a secret. You and I are in love."

"Who in their right mind would believe that?"

"All of the obvious signs are there. Look at our time together. We have lunch together. Let me hold your hand so they can all see that."

"No, you crazy loon."

Tom recalled when Adele had described him the same way. "Then how about another hug before we go in to have lunch?"

"A little one."

"No such thing."

He hugged her and wheeled her to the dining room. During lunch, she talked about her husband and the convenience store, many of the stories she had already told him early on. There was no mention of the secret. After lunch, he took her back to her room for the nap.

It was no surprise that Delores was in the book alcove. "You'll never guess what happened," she shouted just as he was about to hug her.

"What?"

"A man came here for a book and asked me to help him pick one out."

"Wow! See, good things can happen."

"I never thought it would happen."

"Another reason to enjoy today as the journey to tomorrow."

So, it did not take much after all for a full mood change for Delores. A kind act immersed her in the world she loved and felt useful in. That worked better than any medication. So much so that Tom did not have to hug her after they talked for an hour. She hugged him.

FORTY-ONE

The months passed, marked by some major developments. Mac and Deacon were married in a small ceremony attended by Tom, Shelby's grandparents, Mac's mother, Gloria and Win and a few other friends, as well as some close relatives. Tom was made an honorary father-in-law to Deacon and grandfather to Shelby.

Gloria became a licensed detective at the agency, splitting her time there and at the funeral home where her father came out of retirement to run the business. She moved in with Win at his home after he had taken her to Savannah to meet his family. He had never brought a woman home before. They became formally engaged shortly after that.

Florence was so appreciative of all the good that Tom was doing at the home that she offered him free room and board to be at the home permanently to allow him full access at all times to the residents. He jumped at the chance, and was still able to go to the office a few hours most week days to oversee the Angels at work and play.

When Tom told April of his moving to the home she seemed to take it in stride as another manifestation of his restless spirit leading to anywhere and nowhere. She also told him she was dating a man she had met. Tom wished her happiness.

Tom telephoned Ellie and offered to give her Adele's ashes. He suggested that instead he could plant a tree behind the nursing home and scatter the ashes around its base. Ellie thought that was a good idea, and she and Candice drove there on the day Tom planned to do it. The three held hands and cried, each recalling warm memories. A person can still be special even to just a few people.

Shortly after Tom had established his presence in the home, Ellen and Delores died. He was able to be with them in their final hours and was heartened to be so. They both were aware that someone was there holding their hand and weeping for them. Ellen never did reveal her secret and whatever it was died with her. It would forever remain a secret. He did not converse regularly with Leon, but they did chat at random times and Tom observed that he was friendlier with others than he used to be.

Tom quickly grew close to many of the residents, and they in turn reached out to him. Unlike the disinterested neighbors at the retirement village, these folks were eager to talk about life, chances, and choices in the shortened journey to tomorrow. Perhaps, it makes a difference when the specter of death moves out from the shadows to rest on one's shoulder. A certain clarity brings an outlook of where one is in the scheme of things and this prompts analysis. The haunting misgivings of a spent life fosters conversation on a variety of subjects. Tom particularly relished talks on dreams and their meanings because he could easily relate that to his own experience. Dreams can lead to an assortment of interpretations, and for old folks a dream can open the lid to what happened and what might have been done about it. He also concluded what he always suspected, old folks can easily rekindle romantic notions when they dream and talk about yesteryear experiences of the heart. A few of them even harbored secrets, as did Ellen, and a certain remorse would set in concerning their origin and duration. A vow to keep a secret from a prying world when told to one by another can be a hardship in the closing days when years of loyalty may be tested. If the person who related the secret is gone, are the considerations for revealing the secret different? Does the degree of potential damage or impact change over time? Tom was not surprised about people opening up about the past, both good and bad. He did it himself during periods of self introspection as well as in the long conversations with Mac.

Whenever Mac could free up some time, she would go over to the nursing home to join Tommy in his get together with various folks. She would also do visits on her own, as she found such sessions to be pleasant and rewarding in the sense that she felt she was doing acts of kindness and good. Many of the visits also confirmed what she had thought with Tommy all along. Old people are a national treasure. A number of pearls of wisdom, derived from extended years filled with experiences and lessons, she absorbed in conversations and added to the journal she still kept. It also gave her an insight into the true satisfaction that Tommy derived from his new found mission. For Tom, having his alter ego participating in the venture was comforting and reassuring that upon his own death or incapacitation this endeavor would be ongoing.

So, when all was said and done, the decision to retire from retirement turned out to be one of the best he had ever made. It verified an important lesson. Even for older people, it may not be too late to change the content and direction of one's life. For him, it led to the significant implementation of the plan to help those with a special need in their closing days. In addition, it was the avenue to let two extraordinary women into his life that he loved dearly. Mac was the love of his heart, and Adele was the love of his soul.

Tom's dreams were as vibrant as ever, maybe even more so. They transported him to many tomorrows with meaningful moments winding through and touching the lives of those comprising a vital part of his world. Each journey to tomorrow is fulfilling to the dreamer when the dreams are lived. Such is the kind of secret that can be shared with everyone. It is also the path to a contented life.

www.ingramcontent.com/pod-product-compliance
Lightning Source LLC
Chambersburg PA
CBHW051824170626
46807CB00003B/1015